## 'I know that you're mine for the taking.'

His words frightened Maxi, not because of their intent, but because deep down inside she knew that every single one of them was true. Which made her denial all the more vehement. 'No!'

'Yes!' Kerr corrected emphatically. 'You're fooling yourself if you think this will just go away. It won't. One day or another, you're going to end up in my bed, and we both know it.'

D0718239

**Dear Reader**

Over the past year, along with our usual wide variety of exciting romances, you will, we hope, have been enjoying a romantic journey around Europe with our Euromance series. From this month, you'll be able to have double the fun and double the passion, as there will now be two Euromance books each month—one set in one of your favourite European countries, and one on a fascinating European island. Remember to pack your passport!

*The Editor*

**Amanda Browning** still lives in the Essex house where she was born. The third of four children—her sister being her twin—she enjoyed the rough and tumble of life with two brothers as much as she did reading books. Writing came naturally as an outlet for a fertile imagination. The love of books led her to a career in libraries, and being single allowed her to take the leap into writing for a living. Success is still something of a wonder, but allows her to indulge in hobbies as varied as embroidery and bird-watching.

**Recent titles by the same author:**

THE STOLEN HEART
TRAIL OF LOVE

# AN OLD ENCHANTMENT

BY
AMANDA BROWNING

MILLS & BOON LIMITED
ETON HOUSE,   18-24 PARADISE ROAD
RICHMOND,   SURREY   TW9 1SR

*First published in Great Britain 1993
by Mills & Boon Limited*

© Amanda Browning 1993

*Australian copyright 1993
Philippine copyright 1993
This edition 1993*

ISBN 0 263 78220 4

*Set in Times Roman 10 on 11¼ pt.
01-9309-58560 C*

*Made and printed in Great Britain*

# CHAPTER ONE

IT HAD been a long drive, particularly for someone who was not yet one hundred per cent fit. Maxi Ambro was tired and more than a little nervous, unprepared for the wave of emotion which rose to block her throat as she halted the car and stared at the lovely old house. Long, elegant fingers curled around the steering-wheel as moisture deepened the navy blue of her eyes. Lord, how she had missed this place, the people in it.

She loved them all, but she had hurt them badly more than once in her twenty-seven years—the last time not without cost to herself. At the memory, the face which had launched a thousand ranges of make-up and perfume, with its dramatically stunning bone-structure, teasing eyes and sensually promising lips, froze into an alien sternness.

Time was supposed to be the healer, and seven years was a long time. Plenty of water had flowed under the bridge since then. Enough, surely, to cleanse the past? A tremulous laugh betrayed her uncertainty. She hoped so, because she was coming home to try and sort out the mess she had made.

As she was about to put the white GTI into gear and continue up to the house, her ear caught the unmistakable roar of an engine coming up behind her. In horror she realised that her precipitate stop had virtually blocked the driveway, and the advancing driver had no idea because his view was limited by the vast spread of rhododendron bushes. Even had she not frozen, there would have been no time to move. At the speed the car was going, it was upon her in seconds, and then Maxi could only admire the skill with which the driver avoided what had seemed an inevitable collision, steering his Porsche through the small gap that was left between her and the shrubbery, and back on to the path with a squealing spray of grit.

Coming out of her daze, Maxi followed more circumspectly, parking behind the now motionless vehicle. The car might have been motionless, but the driver most certainly wasn't. He climbed out with the precise movements of a man in the grip of a violent rage. Maxi let out a gasp. He certainly was a magnificent brute, and she'd seen enough men in her time to be a good judge. Over six feet tall, he was broad of shoulder and narrow of hip, each muscle outlined by the clinging cut of his jeans and the silk shirt, which revealed tanned forearms beneath rolled-up sleeves and a hint of dark hair at the open collar. She placed him in his thirties, a living, breathing powerhouse of male sexuality—which right that moment was bearing down on her with the express purpose of putting the silly little woman firmly in her place!

Aware she had been at fault, Maxi sought to appease. Dragging a hand through her ebony hair, she formed her features into their most winning smile and climbed out to meet him.

'That had to be the slickest piece of manoeuvring I've ever seen,' she began, even as her eyes took in the fact that anger in no way lessened the handsome lines of his face. It wouldn't be a soft face; there was too much strength in it, too much certainty that this man knew exactly who and what he was, and didn't have to prove anything to anyone. Except, perhaps, herself, she realised, catching the glint in those flashing grey eyes.

He stopped a hair's breadth away, towering over her, though she was by no means small herself, measuring five feet ten in her bare feet. His chest heaved as he drew in a deep breath. 'So, you think that was slick, do you? Care to give me your impression of this?' he growled fiercely, and, before she had time to do more than blink, he had caught her around the waist, sat down on one of the ornamental urns which bracketed the steps, and pulled her towards him. Before she knew what was happening his mouth had descended on hers.

Her struggle for freedom availed her not at all. He held her easily without breaking sweat, and released her just as easily, setting her on her feet and watching her sweep the hair out of tearful, angry eyes with evident satisfaction.

'Well? Nothing to say?' he mused sardonically.

Nothing to say! So many words were battling for freedom that they choked her! In the end, those that did break free made her cringe in their aftermath, so trite were they. 'How dare you?'

Attractive lips curved in a sneer. 'The typical spoilt brat. Be thankful you weren't a man. I felt like punching you out. What the hell did you think you were playing at? Don't you know better than to block the road like that?'

Maxi forgot her own admission of guilt. As far as she was concerned, he had forfeited an apology by his caveman tactics! 'Don't you know better than to drive around at that speed when you can't see what's up ahead?'

With animal grace, he rose to his feet, thumbs hooking into the belt loops of his jeans. 'This happens to be a private road.'

'Then why were you on it?' she shot back swiftly.

Straight black brows lifted. 'Not that it's any of your business, but I was invited. Were you?'

A small frown cut into her brow. Invited to what? Was her mother throwing a party? Of all the bad timing!

Yet what did it matter that she hadn't been invited? This man clearly didn't know who she was, and she was under no obligation to explain her unannounced arrival to him.

'It just so happens that I don't need an invitation,' she declared with a degree of certainty she was actually far from feeling.

'Is that so?' he murmured, and studied her thoughtfully. When he laughed, it was an unpleasant sound that set out to unnerve her. 'Doubtless it's more comfortable to think that way when you know you'd never get one.'

The assurance inherent in his statement rattled her nerves. 'Just what is that supposed to mean?' she asked shortly, hearing her own tremulousness quite clearly.

Bracing his feet apart, her tormentor crossed his arms and eyed her in icy amusement. 'You don't remember me, do you?'

Startled, she stared up at him. Should she know him? His features were striking, and she was pretty certain she would have remembered them had they ever met. Yet there *was* an indefinable something which eluded her attempts to grasp it. She shook her head. No, if their paths had crossed it must have been at one of the innumerable functions she attended. People, especially men, were often inclined to claim friendship from what had been no more than a polite exchange of pleasantries. However, it wasn't unknown for a man to feel slighted that she'd failed to recognise him. She knew the signs of a bruised male ego well, and his unpleasantness was undoubtedly due to it. Although she wouldn't have thought a man this attractive would be in that class, she put on a professional smile and prepared to pour oil on troubled waters.

'I'm sorry, I didn't mean to cause offence. In my line of business I meet so many people its hard to keep track of names and faces. I'm sure we must have had a very pleasant conversation, and perhaps we can talk it over later, but——'

'Devereaux.'

His interruption halted her mid-flow, and she blinked up at him in surprise. 'I beg your pardon?'

His smile was icy. 'There's no need. Just spare me the bored socialite bit.'

Completely thrown, she could only continue to gawp at him. 'W-what...?'

'Devereaux is my name. Kerr Devereaux,' he went on hardly, his Christian name sounding like the everyday 'car'. 'There's no need to tell me who you are—we have long memories around here. I recognised you at once. Maxi Ambro, the advertiser's dream. Well, let me tell you something, Maxi, you picked one hell of a time to do your prodigal daughter act. Why don't you do everyone a great big favour and go back where you came from?'

Maxi went cold to her heart. If a complete stranger felt this way about her, what would the reaction of her family be? Automatically she stiffened her spine in preparation for the confrontation that was coming. Whatever happened, she wouldn't let this man make her turn tail and run.

'You're right, Mr Devereaux, I don't remember you. But even if I did, you don't have the right to send me away. Only my family can do that,' she told him icily.

'You'd give them the satisfaction of telling you to your face?' Kerr Devereaux studied her stiff figure once more. 'You've got guts.'

If she hadn't had, the past seven years would never have been. 'Isn't there a local school of thought who consider it's what I deserve?' she retorted cynically, allowing a small careless smile to curl her lips.

He didn't like her reaction, that was for sure. 'There is, and I'm a founder member of it.'

Maxi laughed. She could have bet money on that. So, he didn't think she was suitably repentant? Hadn't paid all her dues? He knew nothing, nor ever would. Nor would he ever see her crawl. 'Don't tell me, you're the local Pooh-Bah, are you? Self-appointed, naturally.'

'For someone with a brain the size of a pea, you spout a fine line in sarcasm,' he sniped, straightening.

Her teeth snapped together audibly. 'You're not so bad in the insult line yourself,' she riposted, and caught the flash of his teeth as his smile broadened.

'Well, honey, I tell you, I just look at you and I'm inspired,' he drawled, raking a hand through hair that glinted blue-black in the late afternoon sunlight.

Maxi's patience was becoming dangerously thin. She had been nervous enough without this. Stranger or not, his barbs found their mark. 'Just who are you, Mr Devereaux?'

'So it's true what they say—out of sight, out of mind,' he mocked.

That was the last straw. 'Oh, I've had enough of this stupid cat-and-mouse game!' she declared, and, turning, reached into the back of her car for her case and handbag.

Kerr Devereaux eyed the former in acid amusement. 'A suitcase? I hope you weren't planning on a long stay; you may be disappointed. Or has fame gone to your head? Didn't it occur to you that you might not be wanted?'

Lifting her case, she threw him a glare. 'Mr Devereaux, you are, without doubt, the most obnoxious man it's ever been my misfortune to meet! You clearly don't want my company, so let me relieve you of it!' It was a good line to end on, and with a falsely sweet smile she strode away. Or tried to. Unfortunately her second step brought her on to her left leg. Pain shot through her hip, and with a cry of alarm, she felt it go under her.

Before she could touch the ground though, strong hands caught her under her arms and yanked her upright again. 'What happened?'

The impartial concern in his voice brought colour to her pale cheeks. How stupid to have forgotten her weakened hip! Now she had him to thank for not landing in an undignified heap on the ground. Why did fate have to be so unkind? Pulling free of his hold, she gritted her teeth.

'It must have been a stone. I'm OK now.' Mentally keeping her fingers crossed, she tested her weight on the injured leg and breathed in sharply as it protested.

'Some stone,' Kerr observed drily, slipping a hand around her waist and taking her weight.

'I don't need your help,' Maxi protested, to no avail. 'I can manage!' This as he relieved her forcibly of her case.

Grey eyes lanced into her. 'You can manage to crawl. Is that what you want?'

He knew the answer as well as she did. She'd rather die! 'No,' she gritted out.

Now his eyes danced as he fended off her daggers. 'And they tell me you were such an angelic child. Who'd have thought you'd turn out to be such a bitch?'

Lord, he made her blood boil. 'Haven't you heard that if you can't say something nice about somebody, don't say anything at all?' she sniped witheringly.

'There are exceptions to every rule,' he shot back swiftly. 'How's the leg now?'

Swerved from her intention of lobbing a pithy reply, Maxi tested her weight instead. This time there was no shaft of pain, just the well-known dull ache. 'It's much better,' she said, looking up, and added grudgingly, 'Thanks.'

He watched her take a few experimental, limping steps. 'So, what happened to your leg?'

Rubbing at the aching joint, Maxi sighed. 'I was in an accident a couple of months ago. The brakes failed on my car.'

Kerr's frown of concern was genuine. 'This one?' His finger jabbed at the white convertible.

'Hardly,' Maxi admitted with a wry laugh. 'That was a write-off. I was lucky I just hurt my leg.' Something of an understatement, when it had been broken in several places. 'I had to get this automatic because I still can't put too much strain on my leg. As you may have noticed. It plays up when I've been sitting or standing too long.'

'You're lucky it wasn't your face,' he observed, and her smile faded.

'Wasn't I?' she agreed, unaware that her too composed features revealed more than they concealed. All she did know was that nothing happened without a purpose. It had been a kind of short, sharp shock, making her take stock of her life and where she wanted it to go. But before she could go on, the past had to be laid to rest.

Which brought her back sharply to the present. 'Where is everybody?' she thought to ask rather belatedly.

'Out on the terrace, I should imagine,' Kerr Devereaux offered, setting her case and handbag aside. 'You'd better leave those here for now. We can go round the side.'

'You seem to be pretty familiar with the house. And you still haven't explained who you are,' Maxi challenged as he took her by the arm and steered her around the building.

'I'm familiar with it because I'm a frequent visitor here. As for who I am...' His voice took on an odd inflexion. 'You'll find out any minute now. I wouldn't want to be in your shoes when the flak starts flying,' he added cryptically, and said no more.

Maxi's shoes beat a staccato tattoo on the stone flags as she walked beside him, mind seething with question, but as they came round to the back of the house she stopped wondering who he was and concentrated instead on the group of people on the terrace. If it was a party, then it was a very small one. As yet, none of the four had heard their approach, and she was given a few seconds' grace to study the three members of her family. Her heart contracted. Her father looked so much older. His hair had turned grey and there were deep lines on his intelligent face. Beside him, her mother looked very little altered, save for two wings of grey at her temples.

Maxi didn't recognise the good-looking young man who stood with his arm around her sister's shoulder. Fliss had matured in the last seven years, turning into the beauty she had always promised to be. She was smiling up at the man, and the look in her eyes said it all. So did the look in his. They were in love, and Maxi suddenly felt like bursting into tears. Tears of mingled sadness and joy, because this was what she had one day hoped to see.

However, there was no more time for thought, because their approach had been detected. Four smiling faces turned their way, and three smiles faded instantly. The shocked silence that fell hit Maxi like a blow, even though she had been expecting a strong reaction. It seemed from a very long way away that she heard Kerr Devereaux speaking.

'Sorry I'm late, everyone, but I found a visitor on your doorstep.'

If he had said he'd found an unexploded bomb, she doubted if the shock to her family could have been greater. Their reaction to that shock varied greatly. Sir John Ambro, after remaining frozen, pointedly turned his back and walked into the house without another word. It was a slap in the face that Maxi had expected years ago, but not now, and she caught her breath sharply. As she watched, her mother ran a distracted hand through her hair and turned anxious eyes on her youngest daughter. As well she might, for Fliss had gone rigid, her whole expression one of utter revulsion.

'What are you doing here?' she demanded coldly.

'Now, Felicity, darling, that's no way to talk,' Lady Ambro reproved, albeit in a shaken tone, watching the once happy gathering disintegrating around her.

Fliss banged down the glass she had been holding. 'Of course it is. If she's back, it can only be to cause trouble! Why else would she pick today of all days?'

'Hush, darling,' her mother said again, and turned to her other daughter, fixing a shaky smile to her lips. 'Maxine, you've given us all such a surprise.'

Maxi could feel herself begin trembling badly, as much from tiredness as pure reaction to her reception. She knew Kerr Devereaux must feel it too, for he still had hold of her arm. Although she would rather it were anyone else, she welcomed the tightening of his hold in grudging support. 'I would have telephoned to let you know I was coming, but——'

'You knew you'd have been told not to bother,' Fliss interrupted scornfully, and not without a certain amount of truth. 'Oh, why couldn't you have just stayed away for good?'

It was a question that reduced everyone to silence. Almost, that was.

'Would somebody mind telling me what's going on? I thought this was supposed to be a celebration?' the young man at Fliss's side asked in bewilderment.

Fliss, her lips trembling, turned her face into his shoulder. 'It was, until *she* arrived.'

Still patently all at sea, he placed a protective arm about her, staring at Maxi. 'But who is she? She looks familiar. Do I know you?' This last was a direct question that Kerr Devereaux chose to answer.

'It seems to me that introductions are in order. Believe it or not, Andy, this is the very same Maxi Ambro you were at school with. Maxi, meet Dr Andrew Devereaux, my little brother and,' here he consulted the gold watch on his wrist, 'as of fifteen minutes ago, your future brother-in-law.'

It seemed it was destined to be a day of shocks, for as Maxi stared at the man who as a boy, she now recalled, had bedevilled her early school days, he was gaping at her. Her fame, it seemed, had gone before her.

'So you're...'

'The black sheep of the family,' Maxi finished for him, finding defence in attack.

To her surprise he shook his head and smiled broadly. 'Actually I was about to say that you're the famous model we see everywhere. I never connected the name with the terror I knew in school,' Andy declared, and reached out his hand. 'Pleased to meet you.'

One out of five wasn't bad, Maxi thought wryly, shaking his hand. Yet she wondered. Could he really be that genuine? Could he really not know who and what she was, what she had done?

'She's changed a lot,' Kerr observed drily, releasing Maxi to go and greet his brother's fiancée.

'I'll say!' Andy declared with an infectiously boyish grin, to which Maxi couldn't help responding with a laugh, and Fliss with a wailing cry as she tore herself away from Kerr and fled indoors. 'Fliss?' Andy called to her departing back. 'Darling, what's wrong?' When he received no answer, he turned to his brother for elucidation.

Kerr obliged with withering scorn. 'Andy, for a doctor, you can sometimes be a totally insensitive clod. Maxi is Fliss's sister. Her *only* sister.'

Maxi's smile was instantly wiped away, and, even though her shoulders wanted to sag tiredly, she braced them into something worthy of an army recruit. If there was any advantage to be gained by getting in first, she was determined to take it.

'Andy, what your brother can't wait to tell you is that I'm the one who stole Fliss's other fiancé from her, virtually on the eve of the wedding.'

# CHAPTER TWO

THERE followed another of those fateful silences, which seemed to drag on until Maxi's nerves were at screaming pitch. She was very much aware of her mother's anxiety and Kerr's amusement. What she didn't expect was Andy's matter-of-fact question.

'Do you make a habit of stealing other women's men?'

Taken by surprise, she gave a delighted laugh before uttering an amused denial. 'No!'

'I'm glad to hear it,' he replied soothingly, ignoring his brother's snort of disgust. 'Now, wouldn't you be better sitting down? You appear to be in some discomfort.' An observation which immediately made her the cynosure of all eyes as, with his help, she hobbled to the nearest chair and sank on to it gratefully.

'Why, Maxine, you're limping!' Lady Ambro declared in concern, and Maxi, who hadn't wanted to call undue attention to her injury, hastily reassured her.

'It's nothing to worry about, Mother, just the lingering results of an accident I had a few months ago.'

'Were you prescribed pain-killers?' In the blink of an eye, Andy had donned his doctor's mantle.

'I have some in my bag,' Maxi confirmed, looking around for it before she remembered Kerr had left it with her case.

He was ahead of her, a wintry smile curving his lips. 'I'll go and get it for you. Andy, I suggest you stop fussing over Maxi and go and see what's happening to Fliss.' It was a gentle enough nudge, but Maxi heard the steel behind it. He didn't want his brother within a country mile of her.

Andy took it at face value. 'You're right, I should have followed her. But I could see Maxi was in pain, and I was distracted.'

An unfortunate admission at which Kerr's expression became grim. 'Well, by all accounts, Maxi always was a distracting little devil. However, you can safely leave her to our tender mercies and go take care of my future sister-in-law.'

Although Andy grinned, he must have picked up something in his brother's tone, because the smile didn't reach his eyes. 'Big brother has spoken. I'll see you later, Maxi. You will be staying, won't you? We're going out to dinner tonight, and there's a party tomorrow. All the family are invited.'

Though she couldn't explain why, Maxi automatically glanced at Kerr. There was absolutely nothing to be read in his face, and that was telling enough. He wanted her to refuse. He wanted her gone, but a perverse devil wouldn't let her make it that easy. It had taken a lot to come here, knowing how she might be received, and he certainly had no authority to insist she go. Therefore she sent Andy one of her famous smiles. 'I'd be delighted to join you,' she agreed, and watched him hurry away, aware of the contained anger of the man at her side.

'Well, you certainly know how to break up a party,' he said shortly, and it didn't take much for Maxi to mentally add on the rider, As well as marriages. 'I'll go and get your bag.'

'Bring it to the rose bedroom, Kerr. Maxine needs to rest,' her mother called after his retreating back.

Maxi sighed. It hadn't been an auspicious start. Her father had turned his back on her, Fliss had departed in tears, and Kerr Devereaux had disliked her on sight. Strangely enough, if the first two had served to undermine some of her confidence, the latter had had the reverse effect. He was the only one who had no right to judge her, yet he had and was at pains to let her know it. Which was a very big mistake on his part, because now more than ever she was determined to stay.

Pushing herself to her feet, she smiled wryly at her mother. 'He's blunt to the point of rudeness, isn't he? He wants me to go, and he has a point. Was it a mistake to come? Would you rather I left, too?' Mr Holier-than-thou Devereaux couldn't chase her off, but she'd go if it was what her mother wanted.

However, Lady Ambro shook her head adamantly. 'By no means! I know it gave me a shock to see you, Maxine, but that was because I'd more or less convinced myself I wouldn't see you again.' With a watery laugh, she hugged her daughter to her. 'I'm glad I was wrong. I missed you when you cut yourself off so completely.'

Swallowing back tears, Maxi found her voice. 'After what happened, I thought it was for the best.'

Holding her at arm's length, her mother sighed. 'I understood that, but when you went to the trouble of writing to tell me of your divorce I thought you'd surely visit.'

Maxi shrugged helplessly. It was hard to explain when there was so much she couldn't say. 'At first I wouldn't, and then, later, I couldn't. I'm afraid I was a coward. I knew I'd hurt you all, but although I wanted to come home, I couldn't face the thought of being turned away,' she admitted honestly.

Her mother clucked her tongue sadly, not denying the truth of the statement. 'What made you change your mind?'

Automatically Maxi rubbed her thigh. 'The accident. It made me realise how precarious life is. Had it been worse, I might never have had the chance to come back and say how sorry I was. It was time to stop being so cowardly. So I made the decision, and here I am.'

Linking her arm through her daughter's, Lady Ambro shook her head chidingly. 'You, a coward, Maxine? But you were never one to back away from a fight! Nor have I ever known you to fail to do what you knew to be right, whatever the cost,' she declared in surprise. 'That's why you came today, and that's why I won't let you go again so easily. Yes, you hurt us, but you're still my daughter, and I love you.'

'Oh, Mother, you make it sound so easy, but you know it isn't going to be,' Maxi exclaimed with a shaky laugh.

'Of course it isn't, but you were already prepared for that, weren't you? Both Felicity and your father will come round in time,' she pronounced positively, leading them slowly into the house to where the graciously curved staircase swept upwards to the second floor.

About to mount it, footsteps behind them made them halt and turn around. It was Kerr with her luggage.

'I'll look after Maxi, Bernice. There's no need for you to struggle upstairs just to show her her room.'

Maxi's heart gave a severe jolt at that, but there wasn't time to refuse, because her mother was already releasing her.

Lady Ambro sent him a warm smile. 'That's kind of you, Kerr. As a matter of fact, I would like to go and find John. We'll have a talk later, darling,' she promised, smiling at her daughter.

There was nothing Maxi could do but put a brave face on it, and allow Kerr to take her arm in an altogether different sort of hold. She had the uncanny feeling he was debating the possible repercussions if he tossed her down the stairs! It wasn't a comfortable sensation, and she tried to defuse it. 'Why didn't you want Mother to go upstairs?' she charged curtly, and received a scornful glance.

'Had you bothered to keep in some sort of contact, you might know your mother suffers from arthritis. It's playing her up today, although she'd be the last to admit it.'

He had the damnable knack of hitting her where it hurt most, reminding her just how little she knew about her family now. She was left grinding her teeth in impotent rage as they reached the landing and turned down the corridor. If she was silent, Kerr was disposed to be chatty.

'You realise your father was very hurt by what you did, don't you, Maxi? Your whole family were. He couldn't get over the disgrace of knowing a daughter of his could cause such a scandal. The consequence, as you saw for yourself, was that he swore he would never speak to you again.'

Maxi halted abruptly, sending him a killing look. 'I realise you don't like me, but there's no reason to sound so pleased about it!' she muttered, using anger to mask her hurt. God, he was enjoying himself!

His mouth twisted mockingly. 'I'm surprised it bothers you. You are, after all, a totally selfish, amoral little bitch. However, this isn't meant as a condemnation, merely filling you in on a few things. You see, I'm afraid his anger didn't stop there.'

Maxi lurched from one breathtaking insult to another like a piece of disintegrating flotsam. Finally she rallied with a determination never to let him see just what damage he was causing. 'If you mean he had my name expunged from the family bible, I'd pretty much worked that out for myself!' she retorted with an edged smile, which told him to do his worst but not to expect blood because she was impervious to his cuts.

Eyes gleaming, he took up the challenge. 'Did he? I wasn't aware of it, but it doesn't surprise me.' Going to a door along the corridor, he pushed it open. 'The rose bedroom,' he introduced, standing back to allow her to enter, his whole attitude one of anticipation.

Maxi stepped forward before comprehension struck her. She was only grateful he couldn't see her face when she realised the rose bedroom had once been her own. She halted in the doorway, aware that more than the name had been altered. It was a beautiful room, but nothing remained of the former occupant. Not only had the décor changed, but so had every stick of furniture.

'He had it done straight away. There was no stopping him.'

Her heart squeezed painfully at the realisation of just how hard her father had tried to wipe away the memory of her. It made no difference that she had known how much she would be hurting those she left behind; she had never expected to see the result of it. But she had, courtesy of Kerr Devereaux. She could never hate her father for what he had done, but she could and did experience a great welling of hatred towards the man who waited silently behind her.

Walking inside, she carefully composed her features before facing him. 'You know, you missed your calling,' she declared conversationally, as if she found him amusing. 'I imagine you would have been a whiz as a torturer. You get such pleasure from your work!'

'Marriage to Ellis wasn't all you expected it to be, was it?' he said by way of an answer, following her inside and closing the door.

Maxi gasped, then simply had to laugh at his sheer effrontery. She could never remember anyone speaking to her like this in her whole life! She stared at him in awful fascination. 'Doubtless it won't astound you to hear it was no bed of roses?' she queried wryly. She had, after all, gone into her marriage with her eyes fully open, and it had lived down to her expectations of it. 'A piece of news which will cheer Fliss up no end!'

'Not nearly as much as to know that you've gone,' he rejoined instantly, and once again she was forced to laugh.

'She certainly has a champion in you, doesn't she? Are you sure you're not the teeniest bit in love with her yourself?' she taunted, and had the satisfaction of seeing him breathe in sharply for a change.

Kerr's wrath spanned the space between them in a flash. 'That's about the level of remark I'd expect from a woman who'd steal her sister's fiancé.'

Maxi went to the window, brushing aside the net, feigning an interest in the view. 'As you've assumed you can say what you like to me, I've taken the same option myself. If you begin to find it irritating, you can always stop,' she advised, letting the curtain drop and turning to lean casually against the frame.

'I take it from that remark that you're staying, then?' he observed caustically.

Clearly he wasn't about to take the hint and put up his weapons, and she found his continued animosity very wearing on her nerves, not to mention her temper. 'It would seem so,' she replied with a bland smile.

Grey eyes narrowed. 'What have you come for, Maxi?'

This time she raised both eyebrows in mocking rebuke. 'Surely that's my business, and my family's?'

He shifted his weight, and the act of slipping his hands into his pockets drew her eyes to his legs and the way the material stretched across powerful thighs. To her chagrin, deep inside, the feminine core of her twisted in instant response. Defensively she averted her eyes, annoyed that a reaction she hadn't experienced for so long should have been brought about by him. It also left her with a much more rapid pulse, and she desperately hoped she hadn't betrayed herself in any way. It appeared not.

'You're forgetting that, as of today, our families are linked,' Kerr reminded her unnecessarily, coming a step closer.

It produced an unnerving reaction in her, making her suddenly feel as if she was being hemmed in, and that there was very little air in the room. She was forced to turn away, making quite a performance of opening a window, thus giving herself time to recompose her features. 'All right, I'll rephrase the question. Why do *you* think I've come?'

He didn't hesitate. 'To cause trouble.'

Her laugh was brittle even to her own ears, revealing just how much her response had shaken her. 'Thanks for the vote of confidence! Is it so impossible to imagine that I've simply come to see my family?'

'Frankly, yes. You've already proved yourself to be a calculating woman when you stole your sister's fiancé. And don't pretend you couldn't help yourself. You knew what you were doing, every step of the way,' Kerr insisted derisively.

If she had any explaining to do, it most certainly wasn't to this overbearing stranger! Her chin rose an inch. 'You're absolutely right! I wanted to take him from her, so I did!'

Kerr shook his head slowly, eyes registering a boundless contempt. 'You've no remorse, have you?'

Her lashes dropped, shielding her thoughts. 'None. What else would you expect? I will never, ever, be sorry that I took him away,' she added for good measure, knowing that, in his blindness, he would never think she could be sorry for anything else. Besides, her statement was true.

'And you want me to believe you haven't come to cause trouble?' he sneered, and Maxi clenched her hands into angry fists.

'Actually, I don't expect you to believe anything. What you do or don't think is totally immaterial to me.'

He took a threatening step towards her, finger stabbing out to emphasise his words. 'Maybe so, but remember this, I'm not about to let you start another scandal. So if you've got it in mind to have yourself a little fun at other people's expense, do yourself a favour and forget it. Try anything, and I promise you'll live to regret it.'

Arms akimbo, she squared up to him. 'Just what do you think I'm going to do? Didn't you hear me tell your brother I don't make a habit of taking other women's men?' she charged.

'Women have a habit of saying one thing and doing another,' Kerr pointed out tersely, and Maxi sent him a withering look.

'You're saying men don't? I know someone who'd give you one hell of an argument!' She'd spent a lifetime with him, the summer of their brief marriage. Colin Ellis had had one unbreakable rule: never tell the truth unless it was unavoidable.

Kerr seemed unimpressed. 'Let's just say I'd be more inclined to believe a man than a woman.'

A statement that explained a lot. 'What happened? Did a woman let you down? With your attitude, I can't say I blame her!' Maxi jeered.

There was a fleeting instant when he looked positively murderous, then it was gone just as quickly, leaving her wondering if she'd imagined it. 'You'd like that to be true, wouldn't you? However, before you get into your stride, it's only fair to tell you you're barking up the wrong tree,' Kerr denied smoothly.

Maxi raised her eyebrows sceptically. 'Really? I don't believe you. You see, I'm more inclined to believe a woman than a man.'

He smiled, but without a trace of humour. It more closely resembled devilish delight. 'Personal experience?'

She pulled a face. 'There's nothing like it.'

Reaching out a hand, Kerr trailed a finger along the curve of her cheek. 'Poor Maxi. From pampered pet to the school of hard knocks. Why do I find it so hard to feel sorry for you?' he derided.

Feeling bombarded from two very diverse directions, Maxi jerked her head away from a touch which had seemed to scorch her flesh. 'The very last thing I'd want from you is your pity! Now, if you wouldn't mind leaving, I'd like to rest.'

Much to her relieved surprise, he turned on his heel without argument, only pausing at the door to let off his parting shot. 'I'll go for now, but I'll be watching every move you make until you leave,' he warned, and went out.

A fact Maxi didn't doubt for one minute. She only began to relax when the door closed behind him, acknowledging with a shiver how tense the atmosphere in the room had been. His animosity was almost a palpable thing, leaving her in little doubt of his feelings. She didn't like to be so deeply disliked, especially by someone who didn't know her, but, as her feelings virtually mirrored his, this time she didn't care. Kerr Devereaux could go to hell with her compliments!

Sighing, she slipped out of her suit and went into the bathroom to wash away the grime of travel. By the time she returned, feeling much more comfortable, she found a tray of tea had been sent up. Finding her pain-killers, she swallowed one before fluffing up the pillow and stretching out on top of the bed, sipping at the reviving brew. As the ache slowly faded, her thoughts drifted to the last time she had sat in this room. She had been about to make the most momentous decision of her life, and one from which she was still feeling the repercussions.

Even after seven years she couldn't think of Colin Ellis without having to repress a shudder. She had met him at a charity function hosted by the fashion industry. With her modelling career just reaching the dizzy heights, she had found it quite flattering to receive the attention of such a handsome man, and the younger son of an earl to boot. She had dated him for several weeks, gradually becoming aware that he was obsessed by her. She had found that frightening and unhealthy, added to which she hadn't liked the people he called friends, and had begun to suspect he dabbled in drugs and other things she wouldn't give the time of day to. She had broken off the relationship with relief.

Only it hadn't ended there. He had refused to take no for an answer, badgering her day after day, until she'd seriously considered going to the police. But then he had stopped—just like that. She hadn't heard from him again. Which was why she had had no idea of the shock in store for her when she went home to Dorset for her sister Fliss's eighteenth birthday. Then the reason for his absence became obvious, because Colin had been at her home, and, furthermore, was engaged to her sister!

It had been the beginning of a nightmare. When she had tackled Colin, he had been only too happy to tell her he didn't want Fliss but had used her to get to Maxi, the woman he really wanted to marry. Maxi, he had said, could stop the marriage any time, by agreeing to take her place. If not... He had gone on to detail exactly what he had in mind for Fliss, and a wedding ring hadn't been part of it. Also, should she repeat the conversation, he would deny everything. The choice was hers.

Feeling trapped, she had first gone to her father, but her efforts to make him see the truth and refuse the marriage had failed because, since she was unable to support her claim, her statement that Colin wanted her not Fliss had merely sounded like the ranting of a jealous woman.

With very little time, Maxi had hired a private detective to check Colin out. That report had revealed he had once or twice shown signs of a violent temper, was suspected of taking drugs, and was rumoured to carve a notch on his bedpost for every new conquest.

Her worst fears realised, Maxi had done her best to persuade Fliss to break off with him, but Fliss had absolutely refused to believe anything against him. Colin wasn't like that. Maxi was only jealous because she, Fliss, had taken away one of her admirers. The argument that had followed was destructive, and Fliss's wilfulness shocked Maxi. She had never realised quite how jealous and inferior her sister had felt. Maxi had never been vain of her beauty, nor of the way men had always run after her, but it had been salt in the wound for Fliss. Now, having at last put one over on her sister, Fliss had been determined not to lose her victory.

When a discreet visit to the police had failed, because there was nothing they could do, no charge they could bring, she had seen only one thing to do. She had to stop the marriage, and there was only one sure way of doing it and making sure that Fliss fell out of love with Colin at the same time. With no help to be gained from outside, she had had to rely on herself. Her sister's happiness meant more to her than her own, and, though she knew Fliss would hate her for what she was about to do, she had hoped that in time she would come to understand and forgive her.

So she had set out deliberately to lure Colin away. He had responded to her flirting and teasing with alacrity, because he understood what it meant. Maxi felt nothing but disgust for him, but had discovered an unsuspected talent for acting. To universal condemnation, she had refused to stop, although pretty soon she was the talk of the neighbourhood. She had steeled herself to ignore Fliss's tears, her father's angry disapproval and her mother's anxiety and confusion. The only way was to carry on regardless, even though it had broken her heart to see the way she was hurting the people she loved best in the world.

Unfortunately, her plan had had two parts, one to get Colin away from Fliss, then to free herself. The first part had worked easily, but not the second. Colin had refused to let her out of his sight until she married him. She had thought of running away, but he had told her the threat to her sister hadn't vanished, and wouldn't until the wedding. She had known herself to be trapped, but she hadn't knuckled under, even though less than a week after her sister's eighteenth birthday the pair of them had gone to America together and were married.

Maxi shuddered and drained the last drops of now cold tea from her cup. Some marriages were made in heaven, but hers had not been, and it had proved impossible to walk away unscathed from that kind of marriage. The scars might not show, but they were there, and she had vowed to herself that she would rather spend the rest of her life alone than ever risk adding to them.

One thing alone cheered her: she might be scarred, but she had had her victory too. More than that, the proof of how right she had been to do what she had was in this engagement. Fliss had achieved the happiness she had always wanted for her. And that put a smile on her lips as she closed her eyes.

# CHAPTER THREE

AT SEVEN-THIRTY that evening, Maxi descended to the ground floor and made her way to the lounge. She had dressed with care out of sheer habit, although the prospect of the evening to come would have made her don any armour she possessed. All she had was her make-up and the manufactured smile that any good model soon learnt to project. Fortunately clothes were never a problem. Unprepared as she was for the celebration, it was still second nature to pack at least one good dress in her case.

There was a certain unintentional amusement in the fact that the said dress happened to be scarlet. Freud would probably have had a field day, but the truth was that it was her latest buy. The fitted bodice needed no straps and clung lovingly to a bust that was a little fuller than was usual in a model. The skirt was full, ending a couple of inches above her knees. Around her neck she wore a simple gold rope and on her feet were moderate stilettos in the same shade of red.

Feeling that she at least looked ready for anything, she braced herself to meet the family. Walking through the door, however, she found only one person there, and that a most unwelcome one. Kerr turned from the painting he had been studying and ran a lazy eye over her. Normally that would have irritated her, but his appearance was such a surprise that she found herself doing the same.

Tonight he was dressed formally in a black dinner suit, complete with bow-tie and cummerbund. The change was startling, as her senses registered instantly. The raw power he had exhibited in casual dress was now leashed, and all the more potent for it. This man is dangerous, was the message her brain received. Not in any life-threatening way—this went deeper, to the core of her, by far more subversive means, and, as if recognising a potentially superior foe, her defences rose instantly.

'Are we to assume you're playing the scarlet woman tonight?' Kerr enquired sardonically, raising his eyes to hers, and there it was again, that infinitesimal moment of pure rage. Instantly masked, it was replaced by a gleam that raised the fine hairs on her flesh, causing her to shiver.

Not liking at all the wilful way her senses were reacting to him in spite of her volition, she produced an insouciant smile. 'Why not? Everyone will be thinking it, so why disappoint the public?' she quipped, turning away from him and wandering to the open terrace doors, because once again she was suddenly finding it necessary to have air. Nerves, she told herself irritably, and faced him again. 'What are you doing here?'

He grinned. 'The way you say that, I get the impression I'm not wanted. But you know what they say—you can choose your friends, but you can't choose your relations.'

Maxi widened her eyes. 'But we aren't related,' she pointed out with a certain satisfaction—something she knew he'd noted by the way his grey eyes gleamed.

'Yet,' he reminded her succinctly, and indicated the tray of drinks on the sideboard. 'Can I get you something?'

Deciding she'd feel more comfortable if her hands had something to do, Maxi nodded. 'I'll have a Baileys, thanks.'

Pouring her one, and a whisky for himself, he came to join her. 'You don't have to watch your diet?'

'Thankfully not.' Taking the glass, she couldn't help but touch him, and felt a *frisson* of electricity shimmer up her arm. She only just managed to hold back a gasp of pure shock. It was peculiar how the silence which fell then made her tense up, although it was barely measurable. Feeling unnaturally gauche, she knew she had to break it, and hastily cleared her throat. 'I've been trying to remember Andy at school, but I can't.'

Of course, she had to look at him then, and there was a faint smile hovering about his lips, almost as if he knew exactly how she had been feeling—a realisation calculated to bring warmth to her cheeks, although she refused to look away.

'That's not surprising. He wasn't the handsome devil he is now. He had glasses in those days, a jacket that was too big for him, and permanently grazed knees.'

His description brought his brother to life so clearly that Maxi gave a gurgling laugh. 'Now I remember. He used to call me "Beanpole", and I used to hit him.'

Kerr's smile was wiped from his face. 'So he told me. He remembered you all right. Apparently he had quite a crush on you at one time,' he said flatly.

Maxi sobered instantly. 'Don't blame me for that. All children have crushes. Even you.'

'I'll admit to a certain salacious interest in my old gym mistress. She was a large lady, as I recall. But as I got older, my tastes changed. In fact, I tend towards women closer to my own height—like you,' he finished softly, and took malicious delight in the way her colour fluctuated wildly.

'You're joking!' The thought made her stomach lurch painfully, but not, she was ashamed to admit, from fear.

'As it happens, I'm not. But don't worry, I also feel a need to respect the women I take out, so you fail on at least one count.' He waited until he was sure the hit had gone home before continuing. 'No, what worries me right now is the thought that there might be some lingering embers of the crush he felt for you, just waiting to be rekindled.'

She gaped at him incredulously. 'Don't be silly; he's engaged to Fliss!'

The way his attractive mouth broadened into a wide, knowing smile should have warned her of what was coming. 'Why, Grandma, what a short memory you have! So was Colin Ellis, wasn't he?'

Her head went back, and her lips parted in a tiny gasp of anger, whilst at the same time it surprised her that she actually felt hurt. 'That was different,' she protested hardly.

His look was sceptical. 'Oh? In what way?'

And there, of course, he had her. Even if, for some obscure reason, she should want to explain herself to him, it still had to come after Fliss and her parents. They had the right to hear what she had to say first, if anyone did. Her eyes glittered, signalling her impotent anger, then she shrugged. 'It just was, that's all. I give you my word I have no designs on your brother.'

Kerr sighed elaborately. 'Unfortunately, darling, your word really isn't worth a brass farthing.'

That had her temper rising again, and her eyes flashed her dislike. 'What do you want me to do? Have a document typed up and sign it in blood?' she scoffed, and could have hit him when he appeared to consider it. Then he laughed.

'It has certain merits, and, being a lawyer, I could get it done easily enough, but I have the feeling you'd simply claim you signed it under duress.'

'My God, you certainly know how to hit below the belt, Kerr Devereaux. When I give my word, I never go back on it,' Maxi declared forcefully, only to see that mocking smile reappear.

'Don't I remember a part of the marriage service where you promise to stick by your husband for better or worse?'

He was a devil! No wonder he was a lawyer; he'd run rings around witnesses and enjoy watching them squirm! Her teeth gnashed together. 'That was different, and you know it!'

'The same different as before, or is that a different different?' he mocked back.

Maxi was so angry she could feel herself shaking. 'Oh, for a gun or a knife!' she exclaimed in fury.

Kerr, although he claimed to dislike her, still found her endlessly amusing. 'Fortunately for me, they're just like policemen—never around when you want one.'

That should have sent her temperature off the scale completely, but the odd effect of his quip was to calm her down, and she eyed him in reluctant amusement. 'However have you managed to live so long?'

This time his laughter was genuine. 'Just lucky, I guess. Ah, here come the others.'

Maxi quirked an eyebrow. 'Like the cavalry, always in the nick of time?' she bantered back, and caught a gleam of appreciation in his eyes as they turned to the door.

It was her parents who entered, her mother looking very fetching in a violet silk two-piece, and her father, in dinner dress, looking quite dapper for his age. Almost twenty years older than his wife, he was now in his seventies, but still strikingly handsome. Until fairly recently he had had his own law firm. Maxi recalled that Kerr had said he was a lawyer, and it occurred to her to wonder if he might not have taken it over.

A fact her father confirmed as he greeted the younger man. 'Hello, Kerr, how's the old firm doing these days?' he asked as they shook hands.

'Managing to live up to your high standards, I think, John,' he replied before turning to kiss her mother on the cheek. 'You look lovely, Bernice. You're going to cut quite a swath through the club tonight.'

Lady Ambro laughed delightedly. 'Flattery will get you everywhere, you dreadful tease!' She had already noted her elder daughter's presence but now she remarked upon it. 'Maxine, what a gorgeous dress. You look beautiful. Don't you think so, John?' she appealed to her husband.

Maxi found herself holding her breath as her father was obliged to turn to her. He looked grim and forbidding, without forgiveness. When the silence dragged on, she swallowed to moisten a dry, tight throat.

'Hello, Father,' she greeted huskily. 'You're looking well,' she added, hoping against hope to see a chink form in his reserve.

His expression didn't change for a moment, neither did he speak. The only sound he made was a guttural grunt as he turned back to Kerr. 'Young man, I've been meaning to talk to you about...'

Maxi didn't hear any more; it faded away as sudden tears welled behind her eyes, and she pressed her lips together in a struggle to hold them back. Throat tight, she swung away, knowing it was what she had expected, but hurting all the same. After a moment her breathing eased, and she sipped at the remains of her drink, finding it soothing. Only then did she become aware that her mother had joined her.

'I'm sorry, Maxine,' she apologised. 'I should have known better than to think I could bludgeon him into talking.'

Maxi looked round and smiled, only a slight pallor showing that anything had been amiss. 'Don't worry. I haven't forgotten that Father always did see things as black or white, no grey. Mother, are you sure you want me with you tonight? People are bound to talk.'

'They would talk even more if it was known you were here but hadn't been invited. No, dear, this is by far the best way,' her mother decided, and smiled across the room to where Fliss and Andy had arrived.

Maxi eyed her sister ruefully. 'Fliss won't like it.'

Lady Ambro patted her daughter's hand. 'Perhaps not, but she's old enough now to do what's right. Family should stick together, and any disagreements should be kept strictly at home.'

Andy was crossing the room towards them, towing a patently reluctant Fliss with him. Kissing his future mother-in-law, he grinned infectiously at Maxi. 'Hi, there, Beanpole,' he teased.

With a scowl, Maxi wagged a fist at him. 'Call me that again, Buster, and I'll find some ants and put them down your shirt the way I did last time!' she threatened.

Andy threw up his hands. 'Pax. I couldn't stand it. My skin crawled for weeks after that little stunt of yours, Maxi.'

She laughed. 'Well, it served you right. I was always sensitive about my height.'

'I don't know why, all the boys thought you were great. Legs right up to your——'

'Yes, well, never mind about that!' Maxi cut him off abruptly, glancing sideways at her sister and seeing the gleam of anger in Fliss's eyes. Not directed at her fiancé, it should be noted, but at Maxi. Nor was she the sole audience. Kerr was watching too, and he was far from amused. She recalled what he had said, and, although she still didn't believe it, it caused a niggling doubt to surface, especially in light of what Andy had said.

Diplomatically changing the subject, she smiled at her sister. 'That's a great dress, Fliss. Yellow suits you.'

Fliss refused the friendly gesture. 'Naturally. You aren't the only one with style and good taste, you know,' she said acidly.

Smile becoming fixed, Maxi bit down hard on her tongue, determined not to give the sort of retort that remark demanded. 'I never thought I was,' she replied quietly.

'Unfortunately, her good manners seem to have gone begging,' Andy interposed sharply, causing Fliss to gasp faintly and stare up at him in surprise at the rebuke.

For a moment the pair of them looked about to explode angrily, then Lady Ambro's gentle voice broke in. 'Now then, I won't have any arguments tonight. Besides, we really should be going. Maxine, I'm sure you won't mind going with Kerr. Felicity and Andrew will be in our car, John.'

Having organised everybody to her satisfaction, and averted a row very neatly, Lady Ambro led the way out. The rest of them followed meekly behind. However, once settled into their respective cars, and on their way, Kerr was anything but meek.

'What the hell were you doing? Andy's never spoken to Fliss like that before,' he challenged brusquely.

Having been on the receiving end practically all day, Maxi was in no mood to compromise. 'Then perhaps it's about time he did. There's no excuse for sheer bad manners.'

Kerr spared her a glance from his strict attention to the road. 'You don't think she has cause?'

Maxi expelled an angry breath. 'Once, perhaps, but not now. Not after seven years and when she's just become engaged to another man,' she was at pains to point out.

'All right, I concede that,' he admitted reluctantly. 'But it would certainly help if you didn't take every opportunity to flirt with my brother!' he charged next.

Her chin dropped at the sheer injustice of that. 'Of all the...! It obviously escaped your notice, but I was not, repeat *not*, flirting with Andy.'

A muscle tensed in his jaw. 'Well, it certainly looked like it from where I was standing.'

'Then I suggest that first thing tomorrow you make an appointment with your optician. You clearly need glasses!' Maxi spat back, keeping her eyes rigidly on the road ahead. The next instant she was flinging her hands out to brace herself against the dashboard as he brought the car to an abrupt halt.

Another car roared by them, horn blaring, lights flashing, and Maxi turned appalled eyes to where Kerr sat, fingers tight on the wheel. Almost as if, had they not been, they would have been around her neck.

'Are you crazy? We could have had an accident!'

'I was crazy not to have sent you packing the instant I saw you!' he grated back at her, the look in his eyes making her sit as far away from him as she could. A manoeuvre that he viewed cynically. 'Yes, you're right to be worried. As for my needing glasses, a man doesn't need twenty-twenty vision to know what sort of woman you are. Trouble, with a capital T.'

Maxi shook her head incredulously. 'You *are* crazy. If you really knew anything about me at all, you'd know I avoid trouble like the plague,' she informed him in all seriousness. Her marriage had given her enough of that to last a lifetime.

'If that was really true, then why are you here? Because nothing but trouble can come from it, and you know it. It's already started. I know the signs, don't forget. I saw how you worked last time.'

Now that revelation came as a real shock, and her eyes widened. 'You were there?' she frowned, trying to pierce the fog of time. 'I don't remember you.' He was not the sort of man she would have forgotten, of that she was sure.

'Oh, I was there all right, but you wouldn't have seen me, you were too involved in luring Colin Ellis into your grasp.' His eyes seemed to be looking beyond her, into the past, and didn't like what they saw. 'You were something to see. Everyone could have sworn butter wouldn't melt in your mouth, but were we ever wrong! You came on so hot the air seemed to sizzle around you. The poor fool didn't stand a chance, and neither did Fliss. Unfortunately the fun soon wears off for you, doesn't it? How long were you married—six months? Nine? It couldn't have been more than a year. I don't suppose he felt he could come back to Fliss after that, not that she'd have had him. That really doesn't matter. The point is this: I won't have you playing those sort of games with Andy. He loves Fliss, but she isn't an exotic flower like you. Like any man, he could be tempted away by the promise of your heady perfume and bright colours, without realising how swiftly they fade and rot away, leaving him with nothing except regrets. You could do it, as easy as blinking, but I'm warning you—don't.'

Maxi had listened to his diatribe in a frozen silence. At the time, she had forced herself not to think of the impression she was giving. Her aim had been to salve Fliss's pride by leaving her with someone to hate. Now, to realise that many had seen her as a bitch in heat appalled her, making nausea rise in her throat until she had to swallow it back.

Even though she knew it would do no good, she had to deny it. 'I'm not like that.'

Unmoved, Kerr put the car in gear. 'I wasn't blind then, any more than I am now.'

Behind her eyes, her head began to throb, and she raised a hand to her temple. He was turning a visit that had always been hard in prospect into purgatory. Well, she didn't have to put up with it. 'If this is the way you feel, why don't you just take me home?' she stated in a frigid voice.

In reply Kerr increased speed. 'No way. You inflicted this on us, and you're damned well going to see it through to the bitter end.'

It was the knowledge that he wanted to see her wounded which roused her to fight back. 'You're a bastard.'

He laughed hollowly. 'They say it takes one to know one!'

Maxi subsided then, sinking back into her seat, feeling rather more upset than she had expected. It was one thing to imagine what people must have thought, and quite another to actually know. Yet even with hindsight, she knew she wouldn't have acted any differently. Sighing softly, she thought it was just as well she had broad shoulders and a philosophical disposition. Having played her part deliberately, she couldn't really blame anyone for thinking she was the kind of woman who greedily took what she wanted. Despite what anyone thought, she had done nothing she was ashamed of, and she wasn't going to be forced to hang her head in shame. She'd kept her chin up even if it did invite certain people to take a swipe at it!

In that fighting spirit she climbed from the car when they arrived at the country club. It was busy, being Friday night, but Maxi was used to such crowds and being in the spotlight. She slipped easily into the smoothly polite façade she usually kept for society occasions. It wasn't the face her real friends saw, but she rather doubted she had many of those here tonight. Kerr kept a firm hand on her arm as he escorted her inside, and she had to admire the aplomb with which he made introductions.

In a country community, where everybody knew everyone else, her fame had gone before her. Their entrance caused quite a stir, and Maxi couldn't help but be amused when the use of her name by Kerr was much like dropping a bomb. The reverberation spread to all corners in seconds. Her lips took on a cynical curve. Those fortunate enough to be here would be dining out on the story for weeks, she thought, and, glancing round to see just how Kerr was taking it, was surprised to see an almost identical look on his face. A laugh bubbled up, and received an answering grin, and, feeling much more kindly disposed towards him, she sailed on. Smiling, she replied politely to any questions asked of her, kept moving on and let the rest pass by.

'You handled that very well,' Kerr complemented, much to her surprise.

Feeling a small glow of warmth in her stomach, she looked at him curiously. What an enigma he was, haranguing her one minute, complimenting the next. 'Thank you, so did you. Considering your well advertised inclination is to side with them, rather than me, I expected to be thrown to the wolves.'

With a hand on her elbow Kerr steered her through to the dining-room. 'That's where you're wrong. I abhor gossip. It's very often malicious and can hurt the innocent. If someone has something to say, then they should have the guts to say it to your face.'

A tiny smile lifted the corners of her mouth. At least he practised what he preached, if the way he spoke to her was anything to go by. 'When you say things like that, Kerr Devereaux, I think I could even get to like you,' she declared in amusement.

'There's no need to go that far,' he retorted ironically, making her laugh.

'I did say *could*,' she qualified, and turned her attention to the table where the rest of the family sat waiting. Sinking on to the seat Kerr held out for her, she smiled an apology. 'Sorry we kept you. I thought I'd forgotten something, and Kerr was just about to turn round when I found it. He wasn't best pleased.' As the lie tripped easily off her tongue, she caught his eye, and although he inclined his head in thanks she knew he was wondering if she always found it so easy to lie.

But she didn't let that dampen her spirits now that she had found a reason to quite like him. However, it did occur to her in passing that he had been responsible for some of the biggest emotional swings of her life to date, but there wasn't time to ponder why he should have had such an effect on her in such a short time.

They ordered their meal and ate it in reasonable good humour. Maxi deliberately took a back seat. This was Fliss's and Andy's night, and she had no intention of spoiling it by a careless remark. Neither, it seemed, did Fliss. Either Lady Ambro had spoken to her in the car, or she had decided to put a brave face on it herself. An onlooker, and there were plenty of those that night, would have said that nothing was wrong.

Afterwards there was dancing, with music supplied by a live band. The newly engaged couple rose at once, followed by Kerr, who graciously swept her mother on to the floor. That left Maxi alone with her father. It saddened her when an uneasy silence settled on them. When she glanced across at him, he was staring down fixedly into his glass of brandy. She decided then and there that the whole situation was ridiculous.

'It's all right, Father, you aren't required to make polite conversation,' she told him with gentle mockery, because she loved him, and didn't want to hurt him any more than she already had. He looked up quickly. 'But if you can bear to listen for a minute, there is something I want to say. Not everything is the way it seems. Sometimes people do wrong things for the best of motives.'

Sir John's eyes, very much like her own, lanced into her. 'Are you saying that's what you did?' he demanded gruffly.

With a sigh, Maxi reached across the table and placed her hand on his, relieved that he didn't immediately pull away. 'I'm saying you might care to think about it. Perhaps even give me the benefit of the doubt instead of condemning me unheard.'

After what seemed aeons, his answer was to ease away from her with another of his speaking grunts. At least, she thought, as the music changed and the dancers returned, he hadn't walked away. Maxi glanced up to see Andy turning to her, clearly intending to ask her to dance. Before he could do so, though, a large male hand clasped hers and drew her to her feet. Even as a protest was leaving her lips, Kerr had drawn her on to the dance floor and into his arms.

'Well, really! You might have asked me if I wanted to dance with you,' she protested rather feebly, because something strange was happening to her insides. She was aware of several things all at once. That the arms which held her were strong yet gentle. That his chest was solid and somehow sheltering. And that her stomach was fluttering nearly as madly as her heart! From a distance she heard Kerr answer, although his breath brushed her ear and sent a tingle down her spine.

'I wasn't going to give you the chance to refuse me. Besides, Andy was about to ask you to dance, and I couldn't be sure you'd say no.'

Instantly her heart settled down into an angry thud and her stomach felt like lead. 'Thanks a lot!' He certainly knew how to make a girl feel good!

'If I was wrong, I apologise,' he murmured mockingly. 'Was I?'

She tipped her head up to send him an icy smile. 'You'll never know now, will you?' And neither would she.

For a while they continued to dance in silence. Maxi had to admit that he moved well. Their bodies seemed to fit together as if they had been made just for that purpose, and it was an unconscious action on her part which had her relaxing against him. Her eyes closed, and she began to softly hum along with the music. It was nice being in his arms like this. No, if she was honest with herself, it was more than just nice. It felt right. Which probably meant she'd had just a little too much to drink, she decided mockingly. Either that, or she was going crazy. She didn't like the man, and the feeling was mutual. So why was it she wasn't fighting to get out of his arms? Just too tired, she lied to herself, with a wry smile.

'Comfortable?' Kerr's husky voice broke into her thoughts.

'Very. You have a very nice body. Everything's in the right place,' she muttered sleepily, and beneath her cheek, his chest rose as he took a deep breath.

'Thank you. You have a very nice body too, and every delectable inch of it seems to be in the right place,' Kerr replied, voice shaking with laughter.

Maxi's eyes shot open as she suddenly became aware that she had spoken her thoughts out loud. Hot colour washed into her cheeks. Good lord, she couldn't have... Her head shot up. 'I didn't mean that the way it sounded,' she denied swiftly.

Even in the subdued light, it was possible to see that his grey eyes were dancing. 'What a pity.'

'Kerr!' Alarm raced through her as she realised he was flirting with her, and she had responded with a tingle of excitement. Hastily she pushed herself a little away from him. She wasn't just crazy, she was insane! It brought a whole new meaning to the phrase 'consorting with the enemy'. If she had given him the impression she was open to offers, she'd have to squash it immediately. 'I meant that we seemed to fit together very well,' she said repressively, before realising that only made it worse. 'Oh, hell!'

Kerr was openly laughing at her. 'This is a mighty strange phenomenon. An apparently sophisticated woman tying herself in knots. Why all the lather?'

'It's you,' she charged, feeling an utter fool. 'You twist all my words round so that I'm afraid to say anything in case you misinterpret it. You must be a whiz in the courtroom,' she added resentfully.

He pulled her back into his arms. 'Will it make you feel better if I admit I was surprised to find I enjoy dancing with you, too?'

Her heart jolted. It did and it didn't. There was something just a little scary in finding there were things about her he liked. She definitely felt safer with a blanket dislike. He was an impossible man! So why was she meekly making herself comfortable again? Was there a streak of insanity in the family? That seemed to be the only answer, because she was also experiencing a strange feeling of *déjà vu*, as if she had been here before, and that was impossible.

'Did I see you talking to your father?'

Whether deliberate or not, with his words the mood changed, and she frowned. 'What a talented man you are. You can dance with my mother and still watch me at the same time!' Unfortunately, she only managed to sound peevish, and, annoyed at herself, her next bid to move away was more determined. However he was far stronger than her, and she was forced to subside or make a scene.

Kerr clucked his tongue. 'You have the quickest temper. The dance was already over, and I only asked because of what Bernice said earlier.'

Pulling a face, she looked up, and, quite without her volition, her eyes filled with tears. 'Damn, I think I'm going to cry.'

With the swift action she was becoming used to, he steered her from the dance-floor and out into the garden.

Away from prying eyes, he pressed a pristine handkerchief into her hand. Maxi promptly blew her nose and blinked back the moisture.

'Sorry about that.' She gave him a self-conscious smile. 'I hate causing a scene.'

Standing between her and the building with his hands in his trouser pockets, he raised his brows. 'That's a good one.'

She stiffened, aware that she had been foolish to let her guard drop. 'Don't start, Kerr. We were getting along fine.'

'Temporarily. You surely don't expect it to last,' he contested.

Expect reasonable behaviour from this man? She wasn't that foolish. 'I may be cabbage-looking, but I'm not green. This is just an island of calm in a sea of storms,' she declared airily.

'Very poetic.'

'Don't sneer, it really doesn't become you,' she reproved coolly.

Kerr looked dubious. 'You've become a judge of that, have you, in just a few hours?'

She shrugged. 'Why not? You judge me.'

'Ah, but I made my mind up a long time ago,' he disagreed softly.

That had been made patently obvious. 'And it would never occur to you to change it?' She couldn't hide her bitterness.

Taking his hands from his pockets, he stepped closer to examine her face. 'Not without good reason. Not when I know... all that I know. Are you feeling better now?'

It was a moot point. 'I'm not about to blubber all over you, if that's what you mean.'

The light caught the flash of his teeth as he grinned. 'You certainly sound better. We'll go back, before they begin to wonder what we're up to.' Taking her arm, he headed towards the door.

Maxi gave a final sniff, 'What's to wonder about? There could be only two reasons for us being out in the garden. The first would have them in stitches. They've probably plumped for murder.'

Kerr halted in the doorway and when she automatically tipped her head up in silent query, he caught her chin with his fingers. 'Why is it so impossible to imagine I might want to get my hands on you for the first reason?' he queried dulcetly, and, before she could guess his intent, he brought his mouth down on hers.

# CHAPTER FOUR

MAXI could still feel that kiss as she prepared for bed. It had been the merest brush of his mouth over hers, but the effect had been astonishing, like being hit by lightning. Her lips had tingled as if they were frozen, yet burned with heat, and every single thought had rushed out of her head. Yet in the midst of it, she had had the strangest feeling of stepping back in time. As if those lips were known to her—and she was sure it wasn't just a reaction to that punishing kiss earlier. But just as she was on the point of understanding, the contact had been broken, leaving her stranded in space.

When, a second later, Kerr had escorted her to the table, she had still been bemused. She must have functioned, though, because she couldn't remember anyone looking at her oddly, and she knew she had spoken, but for the life of her she couldn't recall a word she'd said. Not for those first five minutes. She hadn't danced with Kerr again, but she hadn't refused Andy when he'd asked her to. Not from any sense of defiance, but because, with everyone keeping an eye on them, it would have looked odd if she hadn't.

Unfortunately Fliss hadn't liked it one bit, and showed a regrettably childish inclination to sulk. The evening had broken up soon after that. Kerr had driven her home without comment, accepting her mother's offer of a nightcap when they reached the house. Maxi had refused one herself, choosing instead to say goodnight and go to her room.

Now she slipped out of her dress and reached for the silk robe she had draped across the foot of the bed when she unpacked earlier. Cleaning off her make-up, she heard footsteps mount the stairs, doors open and close, and then gradually the house grew quiet. She was in the act of brushing her hair when she heard a soft tap on her door. Almost she thought she had imagined it, until it came again and she swivelled on the dressing stool.

'Come in,' she invited cautiously, not really surprised to see her sister slip inside and close the door behind her. Fliss was still in the same yellow dress, and had clearly only been waiting for the others to go to bed before paying this visit.

'I want to know what you've really come here for, Maxi,' she demanded without preamble.

Maxi glanced briefly at her sister's hands, which were slowly but surely tearing a handkerchief to shreds. Then she looked steadily into eyes almost the same colour as her own. 'I came because I wanted to see you all,' she said softly.

Fliss pushed herself from the door and took a couple of nervy steps. 'Why? Why now?'

'Because I thought it was time,' Maxi enlarged gently, and, putting the brush aside, rose and went to her sister. 'Fliss, I want you to know I'm very happy for you.' She tried to take Fliss's hand, but it was pulled away.

'I don't believe you. I think somehow you found out I was getting engaged and you came here to make trouble!'

Maxi watched with troubled eyes as her sister paced away again. 'Oh, Fliss, aren't you being just a little bit ridiculous?' she couldn't help saying with some exasperation. 'I'm pleased, really, really pleased. I think you and Andy make a perfect couple. Why won't you believe me?'

Fliss flung round to face her. 'Because I learnt not to trust you.'

Frowning in consternation, Maxi spread her hands. 'But that was seven years ago. Surely what happened in the past has no bearing on this?'

Her sister seemed to be fighting an inner battle. 'I hated you for what you did,' she finally declared.

'I know,' Maxi conceded, wincing.

'I still do.'

Maxi glanced down at her hands. 'I'm sorry. I had hoped we could put the past behind us.' When she looked up, there was a nasty look on Fliss's normally sweet face.

'You weren't happy with him, were you?' she charged gleefully. 'I knew you wouldn't be. I could have made him happy, not you!'

Maxi knew a moment's distaste. 'You're engaged to Andy now. Surely he's the one you should be thinking of making happy,' she reminded Fliss shortly, and watched the colour drain out of her sister's cheeks.

'Oh, why did you have to come and muddle everything up?' she wailed, pressing her hands to her cheeks. 'I was happy! Now you're turning it all into a...a stupid masquerade!' The next instant she spun on her heel and flung out of the room, crashing the door behind her.

Maxi stared at the wood, yet it wasn't her sister's figure she was seeing imprinted there, but the word 'masquerade'. In its commonest sense, it meant a masked dance, and that knowledge had a vice tightening about her heart. She had been to one once, and forced the memory into a room never to be opened. Memory only brought pain. The pain of helplessness. The pain of things that could never be. Yet something had been slowly turning the key. That dance with Kerr, his kiss. She frowned. It couldn't have been him. For Kerr to be that mysterious figure would be too improbable... too cruel.

She shivered atavistically. There had to be some other answer. And yet, there were those inexplicable things. The look in his eyes as if he wanted to do murder. The way he had flirted with her. They made no sense, unless... Oh, but that was too far-fetched. The odds must be astronomical against him being her stranger. She was just being fanciful. There were strong emotions in the air.

Her sister had fairly exploded with them. Years ago, overlooking Fliss's childish jealousy had been a habit, which was probably why she had missed just how deep it went. She might have felt sorry for her once, but not now. In fact, her hand had itched to slap some sense into her. Fliss had absolutely no reason to suppose she was going to set her cap at Andy. Couldn't she see that Andy was a different man from Colin? Didn't she trust him?

Shaking her head, Maxi gave up. Once she had had a good night's sleep, perhaps she'd be able to think of a way of convincing Fliss she meant no harm. Right now her emotions had taken all the battering they could stand. She needed to recharge her batteries for tomorrow. With a deep sigh she changed into her nightdress, climbed into bed and turned out the light.

When Maxi went downstairs the following morning, dressed in jeans and a pink silk blouse, the house was strangely quiet. True, she had overslept a little, but considering there was going to be a large party tonight there was a decided lack of bustle. Mrs Toomey, the house-keeper, was in the kitchen busily polishing silver. She was a new addition to the staff since Maxi had left, and if she was aware of the nature of that departure she gave no sign.

'Good morning, miss. Breakfast is still laid out in the breakfast-room.'

Smiling her thanks, Maxi pushed through the swing door into that room and was brought up short by the sight of long, denim-clad legs stretched out from beneath an open newspaper. In consequence, the return swing of the door caught her squarely on her behind, making her yelp. The paper lowered, exposing Kerr's enquiring grey eyes.

The rest of him was revealed as the paper fell to his lap. Slowly his eyes took her in from the tip of her shiny black hair to her trainer-covered feet. Lingering longest over the shapely length of her legs, he uttered a silent whistle. 'Good morning, Maxi. You're a sight to please the sorest eyes. If you were mine, I wouldn't let you wear anything but trousers—if I let you wear anything at all!'

It was the kind of remark she'd heard all her working life, and she didn't like it any more now than at the beginning. Teeth snapping as her back was put up, she stalked round him to the sideboard and poured herself a cup of coffee. 'Spare me your chauvinistic remarks. I've heard them all before.' Taking her cup and saucer, she deliberately sat down as far away from him as possible. 'You certainly feel free to make yourself at home here, don't you?'

His teeth flashed as he grinned at her. 'If my presence bothers you, you can always disappear for another seven years.'

She loosed a slaying look. 'Very amusing. Have you been practising walking on water? I didn't hear you arrive.'

'Possibly because I never left,' he informed her sardonically.

Startled, her cup halted short of her lips. 'You mean you slept here?' The possibility hadn't occurred to her.

'Can't fool you, can we, Watson?' he taunted.

She sent him a scowl that singularly failed to wither him and gingerly sipped her coffee. The thought of Kerr under the same roof as herself raised gooseflesh all over her, and her lips thinned in annoyance. 'What's wrong with your own house? I presume you have one. I'm pretty certain I recall Andy living somewhere.'

Folding the newspaper neatly, Kerr turned to face her, resting his elbows on the table. 'Yes, I have a house. Unfortunately at this moment it's being redecorated, and reeks of paint and other noxious substances. Your parents kindly offered to house me until my own home was fit to live in again.'

That explained everything. The invitation was exactly like them. Everybody was welcome into the Ambro house. 'Where are they, by the way? Where is everybody?'

'It might be normal for you to laze the morning away, darling, but other people don't care to waste their time,' Kerr drawled, watching her colour rise at his gibe.

Curbing the urge to fling one of her mother's favourite cups at him, she smiled with complete insincerity. 'I didn't ask you for one of your inaccurate judgements. Although, while we're on the subject, I'd say you haven't long finished breakfast yourself, so who are you to throw stones? I asked where my parents were,' she reminded him with a saccharine smile.

'So you did. Let me see . . .' Holding up his hand, he counted off on his fingers. 'John and Bernice have gone in to Dorchester to pick up their engagement present, and various other things that are needed for the party tonight. They dropped Fliss over at the local stables on the way. Mrs Toomey is busy polishing the family silver, and the lady who does is doing the dining-room.'

Having looked at him purely to let him know how much she loathed him, Maxi now found herself becoming mesmerised by the movement of his lips as he spoke. Her heart kicked. She couldn't help but re-member that brief kiss again, and the resulting con-fusion of her thoughts. Could he be? There had certainly been a kind of magic in his lips. But if he was, then that would mean he knew the worst, the very worst about her! That would be the severest betrayal.

'What do you see when you look at me, I wonder?' Kerr mused lightly, but his eyes glittered like steel.

Caught in the act of staring, Maxi's gaze flew to his. She was grazed by his scorn, and her lashes dropped in instinctive self-protection. Could he read her mind? If he knew what she was thinking...but he couldn't. It was just her nerves playing tricks on her.

She made a show of mulling the question over. 'Well, now, what do I see? Do you want the truth, or, like most men, would you rather be flattered?'

Kerr laughed, a husky sound that curdled the blood in her veins. 'Don't spare me. The truth doesn't scare me, because I'm not like most men you know.'

Dear lord, he wasn't like *any* man she knew! They were in the middle of a verbal battle and yet her body was so very aware of him that it tingled! Somehow she had to lower the temperature. 'I see a man who has utter faith in his own judgement. I see a man with the im-placable belief that he cannot be wrong,' she countered coldly, and stifled a groan of irritation when all he did was smile wickedly. His skin had to be made of rhinoceros hide.

'You see that as a weakness while to me it's a strength. But I'm not surprised to find you like to believe the worst of me. Do you think that evens up the scales?'

'Your parents might have spoiled you, but I fail to see why you should have everything your own way,' she challenged coolly.

'Is that why you danced with Andy last night when you knew I didn't want you to?'

Maxi raised her eyebrows pityingly. 'This may come as a shock to you, Kerr, but the world doesn't revolve around what you do or don't want. I didn't dance with him to spite you, but because it would have looked odd if I didn't. Even someone as prejudiced as you must admit that.'

He didn't answer, merely watched her sipping at her coffee. 'Aren't you going to eat something?'

Annoyed, because he wasn't about to give her even that much credit, Maxi shook her head. 'I never eat breakfast,' she informed him, then an imp of perversity made her stir the melting pot just to see what would float to the surface. 'By the way, you left Andy off of your list just now. Where is he?'

In the space of a heartbeat, grey eyes narrowed suspiciously. 'Why do you want to know?'

Maxi sat back in her seat with a laugh, shivering at the way her nerves had leapt with a vicarious excitement. Was this how a bullfighter felt when he had got the bull's total attention? 'What would you like to hear—that I plan to lure him away for a wild orgy of passion on the eve of his engagement party?' Were it another man, she would probably just have made a simple explanation, but she was getting really sick and tired of having her intentions so badly misunderstood. And, yes, to be blunt about it, *wilfully* misunderstood. She chose to ignore the fact that he was only replying to her own devilish impulse.

In a flash he had lurched across the table, catching her wrist in a vice-like grip. 'Try it, you wilful little madam, and you'll rue the day our paths ever crossed!' he threatened chillingly.

Maxi's eyes flashed cat-like. 'I already do!' she spat, struggling uselessly for freedom. 'Damn you, Kerr Devereaux, we were talking about the family. Why shouldn't I idly ask where he was?'

His laugh was humourless. 'Do you ever ask idle questions?'

Her jaw set mutinously, and she absolutely refused to feel any compunction just because she'd got more than she bargained for when she began stirring. 'I did, but you're likely to cure me of the habit. Between you and Fliss, I'm beginning to heartily wish I'd never come.'

He released her then, flexing broad shoulders clad in a black T-shirt, before resuming his seat. 'You have the answer. You can always leave.'

Wouldn't he just love that! 'I'm sure everyone would be delighted, but I'm not going until I've done what I came for,' she refused bluntly.

'Which is?'

'None of your damn business!' she shot back angrily. Getting to her feet, she took great pleasure in ignoring him and stalked back into the kitchen. One of these days, so help her, she'd black his eye for him.

The housekeeper, seeing her thunderous expression, paused in her cleaning. 'Is anything wrong, miss?'

Brought up short by the innocent witness to their private war, Maxi quickly produced a smile. 'Oh, no. Actually I came to ask if there was anything I could do to help.' If she had to rattle around the place on her own, she might as well make herself useful. There would be an added bonus if it kept her away from Kerr, too.

Mrs Toomey smiled. 'If you don't mind getting dusty, there are the two display cabinets in the lounge which need doing out.'

'Consider it done,' Maxi declared, and retrieved polish and a couple of dusters from the broom cupboard before setting to.

Dusting and polishing, she discovered, was quite therapeutic. On her knees, surrounded by various ornaments, her thoughts drifted away to less contentious subjects, and before long she was humming away to herself, quite oblivious to the world around her. Only when something got in her eye did she stop, and as a result become aware that she was no longer alone. With leaping heart, she shot round, to discover Andy grinning at her from his perch on the arm of the couch.

'Oh, God, you fool!' she exclaimed, pressing a hand over her heart. 'You scared the life out of me. How long have you been there?'

'Not long.'

'Do you always creep up on people?'

Andy laughed easily. 'Only when I don't want to disturb them. You looked happy.'

Maxi sank back on her heels and glanced around her. 'I was. I used to do this as a child. It was a special treat then, not a chore, because I'd always end up playing with them. But that was a very long time ago,' she added with a reminiscent sigh.

'Did Fliss used to help you?' Andy queried, coming to squat beside her, fingering one of the pieces.

'Sometimes, but she didn't really have the patience.' Which was only half true. Fliss had wanted to do it because Maxi did, but because she was younger there had been breakages. Consequently, she hadn't been allowed to do it often, and thus another cause for jealousy had arisen. Pausing a moment, she then said softly, 'You do love her, don't you?'

There was no mistaking the look on his face. 'Very much. But I must admit I can't see why your arrival should have upset her so much.'

Neither, to be honest, could Maxi. However, it was second nature to come to her sister's defence. 'You weren't here when . . .'

'The "scandal that rocked the county" took place?' he offered tongue-in-cheek. 'No, I was away at med school. Though news did filter through, I wasn't really interested. Kerr has told me all about it now, though.'

He sent her the strangest look. 'He seems to think you might be up to your old tricks.'

Maxi pulled a face. 'Your brother is long on brains but short on common sense! I don't mean to be insulting, but even if I went in for that sort of thing I'm afraid it wouldn't be with you. I like you too much.'

'Well, that's a relief. I like you, too. I'm a one-woman man, and that woman is Fliss. Nobody could take me away from her.' There was something final and absolute in his tone that warmed her heart.

'Have you told her that?' she asked, rubbing at her eye again as it started to prick.

Andy lowered himself to his knees. 'Of course, but it's up to her whether she believes me or not. I can't force her to trust me; she has to know that she can. Here, let me look at that eye.' Manoeuvring her head into the light, Maxi steadied herself with a hand on his shoulder as he eased back the lid.

To the woman whose silent approach to the door failed to disturb them, the silhouetted tableau was condemning. With a strangulated cry she turned and stumbled away. The two figures by the window jerked round in surprise, but by then the doorway was empty again.

'Perhaps it was a cat,' Andy proffered, frowning.

Maxi licked the handkerchief he held to her lips and sighed with relief when the object, a piece of grit, was removed. 'You don't suppose it was Fliss?'

Tucking his handkerchief away, Andy climbed to his feet. 'No, she would have come in.'

Maxi wasn't so sure. Fliss was behaving so temperamentally that she was capable of anything. 'Was she expecting you to pick her up from the stables?'

Shaking his head, Andy glanced at the clock. 'No. We're supposed to be going to lunch with friends.' As if by arrangement, a loud bleeping sound suddenly invaded the room, and he sighed and pulled an object from his pocket. The noise died away. 'Unfortunately, it looks as if I'm going to have to miss it. Excuse me.' He went to the telephone, dialled and engaged in a brief conversation. Replacing the receiver, he sighed again. 'I was right. I've got to make an emergency call. Make my excuses to Fliss, would you, Maxi, and tell her I'll join her at the restaurant if it's at all possible? Must dash.' With a brief wave, he was gone.

Maxi stared after him, admiring his dedication. Admiring Fliss, too, because she must know what being married to a doctor meant. It was quite a step she was taking. Cheered by these signs of maturity in her sister, she turned back to her chore, but had barely started on it again when a whirlwind tore into the room and swept her to her feet.

'What on earth?' She found herself staring into Kerr's furious face and couldn't help the way her heart quailed. She'd never seen anyone so ready to commit murder. 'What's wrong?'

He looked about to explode. 'You dare to ask me that? When I've just had Fliss come to me in tears?'

Enlightenment dawned. 'Oh, lord, she did see us.'

Kerr's mouth twisted with distaste. 'You admit it, then?'

'There's little point in denying Andy and I were here,' she agreed, and found herself being roughly shaken for her pains.

'Not just here, you damned little... You were in each other's arms!'

Maxi, thoroughly fed up with his attitude, felt her own temper come to the boil. 'Don't you dare keep calling me names! I could think of one or two to call you! Fliss might be silly enough to misconstrue everything she sees, but why do you unquestioningly believe everything she says? We were *not* in each other's arms at all. I happened to have something in my eye, and Andy got it out for me.'

'Oh, come on! That must be the oldest excuse in the book, and the least believable,' Kerr sneered, and Maxi saw red.

Her strength came from somewhere, probably righteous anger, with the result that, having torn herself from his arms, she gave him one almighty shove that sent him backwards. Teetering, he tripped over a stool and went crashing to the ground. Her elation faltered as he lay motionless, and suddenly conscience-stricken that he might have hurt himself, she rushed to kneel beside him. One look told her he was perfectly all right, and concern became anger again. Pinning him down with her elbow on his chest, she used her free hand to point to her eye.

'Look at that, Doubting Thomas,' she ordered fiercely.

Whether because her anger had momentarily subdued him, or because he was temporarily winded, Kerr did let his eyes focus on hers. 'It looks bloodshot,' he finally admitted.

'You're damn right it's bloodshot. It had a lump of grit in it the size of a house brick!' she exaggerated dramatically, still looking daggers at him as he lay beneath her.

Kerr lay motionless, although his eyes began a slow perusal of her flushed face. 'A house brick, hmm?' Something flickered to life in the grey depths.

Her breath caught at the sight of it, and her shrug was stilted as she considered a tactical retreat. 'So I exaggerated. That doesn't alter the fact that you owe me an apology.' She began to push herself up, but in a flash his arms came up and kept here where she was. Looking down into his face, so temptingly close to hers, she felt her heart kick as she saw his mouth begin to curve into a lazy smile.

'I guess I do, but how was I to know?' Slowly but surely he began to exert downward pressure on her shoulders.

A thrill of alarm shot through her, and she tried to brace herself against the floor as she realised his intent. 'There's such a thing as benefit of the doubt,' she managed to say before her throat closed over. He was too strong for her, and her arms began to shake before collapsing. 'No, Kerr!' Her protest came as she tried to avoid his mouth, but a large hand framed her head to hold it still and bring it inexorably down to his.

One touch of his lips and the fight was shocked out of her. It was so gentle, and yet every soft movement was like being stroked by flame, a flame so fierce that it ignited a thousand fires all over her body, bringing senses so tinglingly alive that she gasped at the sheer magic of it. For the first time in years she felt sharply alive, hypersensitive to the intoxicating scent of him, the pleasure in the feel of his strength and the solid beat of his heart.

With a tiny whimper her lips parted to the gentle insistence of his tongue, and then everything changed. No longer gentle, he began a plundering invasion which demanded her response. Suddenly she was burning up, kissing him back eagerly, her tongue taking up the invitation of his erotic caress, her body moving restlessly against his in an ever increasing desire to get closer. Only breathlessness forced her to drag her mouth free, and she stared down at him, gasping in air through bruised lips.

Grey eyes, no longer cold, gazed into hers, and very slowly one eyebrow lifted in mocking question. Sanity returned like a douche of cold water, reminding her just whom she had been kissing, and why it was utter lunacy. Nor was it a moment too soon, for footsteps echoed clearly in the silence and she realised they were about to be discovered. Hastily she scrambled away from him back to the display cabinet, picking up an ornament and replacing it with hands that trembled betrayingly. Mind seething, she was barely aware that Kerr had joined her, and turned startled eyes his way just as her mother walked in from the terrace.

'Goodness gracious, have they got you at it too, Kerr?' Lady Ambro queried with a laugh.

'I'm afraid so,' he answered wryly, clearly having recovered his poise, although there was something savage in his eyes as they held hers. 'Where's John?'

'Parking the car. Oh, we saw Andrew on the way in. Wasn't he supposed to be lunching with Felicity?'

Maxi dragged her gaze from his, hoping she had regained sufficient control of her features when she faced her mother. 'He had an emergency call. Kerr was just about to go and tell Fliss, weren't you?' Her eyes warned him not to argue because she wanted him gone. Unfortunately, her mother intervened.

'Stay where you are—I'll tell her.' About to go out, Lady Ambro paused by the door. 'By the way, there was a telephone call for you earlier, Maxine. A man. He didn't leave his name, but said he would be in touch. Were you expecting a call, dear?'

'No,' Maxi declared in surprise, because as far as she was aware only two people knew where she was, her agent and her neighbour, and both were women. It was certainly puzzling.

'Perhaps it was an old admirer getting in touch, now you're back on the scene,' Kerr observed with a distinct edge to his voice when her mother had gone. 'You must have had quite a few.'

Now they were alone, she allowed her dislike to show. 'But never you. You stayed well away, and as far as I'm concerned the same rule applies now. Stay away from me, Kerr.'

Picking up two ornaments, he held them out to her. 'You wanted an apology,' he reminded her, and she had the distinct feeling he was playing some game of his own with her.

'That was no apology! You just used it to take advantage, and it just served to remind me how much I hate you!' Maxi snapped, snatching the ornaments from him but not being quick enough to avoid having him catch her by the wrists.

'Hate me? Why? Because I kissed you? Or because you enjoyed it so much, you kissed me back?' he taunted, resisting her attempts to break free.

That direct hit wounded her pride. She'd never forgive herself for that moment of weakness, nor him for reminding her of it. If looks could kill, he wouldn't have stood a chance. 'I hate you, Kerr Devereaux, because you only ever think the worst of me. Now get your hands off me before I scream the house down!'

His grip relaxed, but she could tell he didn't really care if she screamed or not. 'Hate away, darling, it doesn't alter the facts. Fliss was in tears, and, as usual, you were responsible.'

Maxi replaced the last ornaments in the case with angry precision and closed the door. Climbing to her feet, she elbowed past Kerr as he followed suit. 'I've told you it was entirely innocent, and I'm damned if I'm going to be held responsible for Fliss behaving ridiculously! So come on, Mr Big Shot Devereaux, why don't you find a way I can convince her I don't want Andy any more than I wanted——?' She caught herself up abruptly, suddenly aware of what she was saying. Cursing herself, she walked over to the other cabinet.

Kerr was no more than a step behind. 'What?' he demanded, grey eyes narrowed and suspicious. 'Wanted what?'

Her eyes slid away from his. 'Leave me alone, Kerr. I'm busy.'

His hand clamped on her shoulder like a vice, spinning her round, and she winced, knowing she'd have bruises there later. 'Not until you explain,' he refused, but as he watched her stubbornly blank face, his own changed to outrage. 'Good God! Are you saying you didn't want Ellis either? That you took him simply to prove that you could? Hell, what kind of cold-blooded bitch are you?'

Stung once too often by him, Maxi flung her head back, eyes wildly challenging. 'The kind you want!' she taunted. She had felt the way his body responded when he held her. Let him deny it if he dared.

'A man's libido has no sense of discrimination. Sometimes any woman will do,' he responded, and his smile was the deepest cut. 'But you, sweetheart, you're saying you don't even have to want the men you take.'

There was no way she could stop herself from paling at his patent disgust. Even so, she fought back. Let him think what he liked, she didn't have to justify herself to him. 'It's no business of yours what I did, or why. The most important thing is that I don't want Andy.'

Kerr released her with alacrity, wincing as if he had a nasty taste in his mouth. 'You are something else!'

Maxi jutted her chin forward belligerently. 'We've already agreed on that, and frankly I'm sick and tired of hearing it from you. Try to be constructive for once. We both want Fliss to be happy, but she won't be unless I can convince her I'm not interested in Andy. Try bringing your legal-eagle mind to bear on that for a change.'

'The obvious thing is for you to leave,' he reinforced bluntly, crossing his arms, 'but you won't do that.'

'I have as much right to be here as anyone. Besides, that wouldn't serve in the long run. I've no intention of becoming a stranger again, which means every time she

sees me she'll wonder. No, it has to be something else.'
Absently Maxi rubbed at the glass as she tried to think.

'There's only one way with someone like Fliss,' Kerr
observed, and Maxi glanced round to find him staring
out into the garden, shoulders as tense as a bow-string.
'She has to see to believe. The only way to convince her
you're not after Andy is to show you're interested in
someone else.'

It was so simple that she wondered why it hadn't occurred to her, but almost at once she discovered the flaw.
'Very clever, Sherlock, but just where do we find this
wonder man?' she scoffed.

He didn't move, but his head slowly turned, eyes
mocking. 'Right here. Me.'

Her jaw dropped. 'You?' Maxi had to force down
hysterical laughter. 'You've got to be kidding!' Pretend
to be interested in him? That would be like...like putting
her head in the lion's mouth, knowing it was hungry!

Now he did move, taking the two steps that brought
him up to her. 'Nobody else would be as convincing to
Fliss. And don't pretend you'd find it a real hardship.
You enjoyed dancing with me, and...' Here his voice
dropped to a husky drawl. 'And you certainly enjoyed
kissing me a moment ago. In fact, your enthusiasm was
most...interesting. I don't see why it shouldn't appeal
to your tastes. You could look on it as a game, and all
in a good cause,' he finished sardonically.

Having heard him describe his proposal so sal-
aciously, she would have to be out of her mind to agree!
'There's no way I'm playing any sort of game with you!'

One eyebrow lifted lazily. 'Why, because it would be
my rules and not yours? You only like playing by your
own rules, don't you, Maxi?'

There was something in the way he said that which
had her pausing before answering. 'The rules don't
matter, because I'm not doing it,' she said breathlessly.

The smile that curved his lips was cruel. 'Oh, but they do matter, darling.' One finger reached out to trace her lips. 'Do you believe in fate?'

Her heart seemed to stop beating. 'What do you mean?'

'It means I didn't want to play the game at all, but sometimes it pays to use the cards you're dealt. You might find yourself holding the winning hand.'

It was crazy talk, but still it filled her with an unknown dread. 'I don't understand you. You're talking in riddles!'

'Then let me see if I can make myself clearer. You're a very good actress, Maxi. I've seen that for myself. You fooled me, and I'm not a man who takes kindly to that. I don't turn the other cheek, I believe in an eye for an eye. Only, with you, I couldn't see my way to achieving what I wanted—until just know. You see, it's all still there, isn't it? Your eyes lied, and your smile, and your words had only a passing acquaintance with the truth, but—and this is the clincher, Maxi—these never lied.' Once again his finger brushed over her trembling lips.

She stared at him, horror-struck. 'Who are you?'

His smile became mocking. 'You know who I am,' he declared silkily, and she paled.

'But you can't be . . .' She couldn't bring herself to say it, but Kerr had no trouble.

'The fool you left behind that night? Oh, but I am, Columbine. Fate brought us together then, just as it has now. Only this time, I'm no Harlequin to be enchanted by your charms. It will be my pleasure to watch you dance to the tune of my choosing.'

When everything seemed to be disintegrating around her, from somewhere came the strength to fight. 'You're wrong. Wrong about everything, and I won't do it!' she choked.

His face closed up. 'Yes, you will. There's no way out.'

Reeling from the shock of his revelation, she shook her head in disbelief. 'The man I knew would never do this.'

Kerr's lips twisted. 'Did he ever really exist? No, it's me you have to deal with, Maxi. But I don't see the problem. You respond to me even if you don't like admitting it. Look on the bright side—you'll be helping Fliss at the same time.'

Only sheer will-power kept her on her feet when her legs were threatening to buckle. 'I hate you!'

He shrugged carelessly. 'That has no bearing on the case. The ball is in your court. If you really mean what you say about Fliss, you'll put your own wishes aside and do it. After all, you want everyone to believe you've changed, don't you? On the other hand, if all you really care about is yourself, well, that will only go to prove I was right about you all along, won't it?' With which pointed rejoinder, he swung on his heel and left the room.

Maxi stared after him in dismay, hating him all the more because she knew he was right. Fliss would believe what she saw. It should have been the perfect solution, but not with Kerr Devereaux. Now she knew exactly who he was.

But he wasn't the man she remembered.

Seven years ago she had gone to a masquerade party. Everyone had been in fancy dress, with almost full-face masks that were to be discarded at midnight. The idea had appealed to her sense of romance, and she had gone as Columbine. The house had been packed with all sorts of characters, but there had been only one Harlequin. Something about him had drawn her eyes to him constantly, sobering her, drying her mouth and increasing the beat of her heart.

She had experienced nothing like it. She couldn't see his face, so it wasn't his looks. But his eyes . . . They had seemed to pierce her to her soul. It hadn't surprised her when he had asked her to dance, nor that, although they said very little, their eyes had held a conversation that blanked out everything else. Words had been superfluous. Struck by magic, she had followed him to a conservatory, going into his arms as if she had always known she belonged there.

Their kisses had held a wonder that anything could be so perfect. Names were unimportant. Everything vital was communicated without words. Maxi knew she had fallen in love, and that he had been moonstruck too. She hadn't wanted the magic to end, but they had been interrupted by a weaving Conga line, which had swept him up and away. She had followed behind, but her eye had alighted on the clock, which showed ten minutes to midnight, and she had known she didn't want to be revealed to him in the midst of all those faces. She wanted it to be private, special. So she had written her telephone number on a card, and signed it Columbine. A passing waiter had agreed to give it to Harlequin, and she had only waited to see him receive it before slipping out of the front door.

She had waited for his call, but instead came the invitation to her sister's birthday party. She had gone to it...and the world she had envisaged had tumbled about her ears. In self-preservation she had locked Harlequin away deep in her heart, making herself forget that one magical evening when the future had seemed bright and boundless. He had remained a memory, until today.

But he wasn't the man she remembered, the one she had preserved in that private centre of her heart. This man had destroyed her most precious memories. This man wanted revenge for being made a fool of. It hadn't been that way, but he wouldn't believe it. So how could she place herself in his hands, knowing how he felt about her now?

# CHAPTER FIVE

BY TEN o'clock that evening the engagement party was in full swing. Maxi took time out from a non-stop round of dancing to catch her breath. She was wearing the same red dress as yesterday. There hadn't been time to go shopping for another, and besides, it looked festive. It was also a statement, to anyone who cared to notice, that she intended to fight on. For the same reason she had piled her hair on top of her head and used make-up more dramatically.

There were very few of the men present she hadn't danced with over the last couple of hours, the exception being Kerr Devereaux—a state of affairs brought about purely by design. Occasionally she had seen him dancing, and had felt his eyes on her more than once, but whenever her antennae had informed her he was around she had moved on, her intention being to keep one step ahead of him at all times. This morning he had deliberately awoken a memory, only to destroy it. She hated him for that, and for the retribution he was determined to claim.

'You've been avoiding me,' an all-too-familiar voice murmured in her ear, and Maxi tensed instantly, cursing whatever fate had caused her guard to drop, before swinging round with a patently false smile.

'Nonsense. There must be all of two hundred people here tonight, so it isn't surprising our paths haven't crossed,' she denied coolly.

Kerr looked sceptical, as well he might. 'The reason they haven't crossed, darling, is because whenever I've made a beeline for you you've hurried away,' he accused, and she laughed.

'I'm sorry if that peeves you, but I'm merely following my mother's orders to circulate. Which reminds me…' Sending him another smile, she went to walk away, only to feel his fingers circle her wrist like a manacle.

Grey eyes narrowed angrily. 'Try circulating *with* me for a while instead of trying to run rings around me,' he commanded, and, when she was forced to subside, sent her a mocking look. 'So, are you enjoying yourself?'

'I *was*,' she declared drily, smiling at an old friend who danced past. 'You can let me go now. I promise not to run away.'

'Perhaps I prefer to keep hold of you,' Kerr argued, slowly running his thumb over the back of her wrist. 'Hmm, you feel good, soft to the touch. It makes a man wonder if you'd be this soft and warm all over. Your pulse is racing. Now why is that, I wonder?'

Racing? It was doing an all-out gallop! His touch and his words had sent heat coursing through her veins, and, though she hated herself for it, she hadn't been able to stop her mind from seeing the erotic picture of his hands stroking over her flesh. Consequently her words had the sting of self-disgust as well as anger.

'Loathing, pure and simple!' she shot back scathingly.

His laugh was a husky note that tripped her nerves. 'Maxi, Maxi, you really shouldn't tell such monumental lies,' he taunted, bringing another wave of hot colour to her already stormy cheeks.

She breathed in sharply. 'The only monumental thing around here is your ego! What makes you think any self-respecting woman would be panting for you?' she charged, and made the mistake of looking up into his fathomless grey eyes.

'Darling, I wasn't thinking of self-respecting women, I was thinking of you.'

Maxi lost her breath and her colour in one go, the wound of his gibe going deep. She was quite literally shaking with anger. 'For your information, Kerr Devereaux, my self-respect is one thing I've never lost.' In fact, she had had to fight damn hard to keep it, when others had tried to grind her down. 'So you'll understand that I'm quite prepared to scream if you don't let me go this instant.'

There was a moment when he simply stared down into her flashing eyes, then his fingers were gone and he stepped back. 'I believe you would, too, even if it meant spoiling your sister's party.'

'There are things I might put up with for Fliss, but not your insults. Now, if you'll excuse me, I have better things to do with my time,' she retorted frostily, and pushed past him.

In pure self-defence she slipped from the room, needing a few minutes' quiet to regroup her ragged army of defences. Instinct sent her down the passage to the library, bolting inside like a rabbit into its hole. Leaning against the door, she sighed raggedly, angrily brushing away the one tear which had escaped. How dared he talk to her like that? She wasn't dirt, and he was a swine even to suggest she was!

'Getting too much for you, were they?'

The dry comment, issued in her father's mellifluous voice, made her jump. There was a click, and a reading lamp spread its mellow glow over the room. Sir John reclined in a high-backed wing chair.

Maxi hastily pulled herself together. 'So this is where you got to.' She had caught sight of him escaping some time ago.

'I'm afraid there's only so much of my fellow man's stupidity I can stomach at one go,' he declared drily. 'Come and sit down.'

The invitation surprised her, but she didn't hesitate to take the chair opposite him. She recalled how many a time she had sat in here with him when she was little, sitting quietly, knowing he would speak when he was ready. It had the comfort of familiarity.

'Are you all right?' There was concern in his voice, and on his face as she found him studying her closely.

Automatically she smiled and shrugged dismissively. 'Just a little tired. It's very hot tonight.' Glancing down at her fingers, her smile became self-conscious. 'Actually I'm glad I found you, Father. While we're on speaking terms, I wanted to say I'm sorry for the hurt I caused seven years ago.'

'Sorry to have hurt, but not sorry to have caused it,' her father enlarged thoughtfully. 'You're trying to tell me something now, even as you did then. I realise now I made the mistake of not listening. I ignored all I knew of you, judging with my pride, and not my heart or my head.'

'Well, you never really forgave me for running away to become a model against your wishes, did you?' Maxi put in wryly. That had been a bone of contention long before the scandal had erupted.

Her father expelled his breath in a long sigh. 'It shouldn't have counted, but it did. I fashioned my own cross to bear, Maxine. Late though it is, I'm listening if you care to explain to me now,' he ended gruffly.

Which was all she had been waiting for. It wasn't a long story, and there were details she chose to leave out. 'I did try to tell you. It was always me Colin wanted, Father. I was his obsession. He used Fliss to get close to me. I tried to get her to see sense, even told her I thought he took drugs, but she was in love, and wouldn't listen.'

'Besides being very jealous of you. Your mother and I were aware of it. We thought she'd grow out of it in time.'

Maxi decided to shrug that off. 'It didn't help. Anyway, to cut a long story short, I decided the only thing to do was take him away from her so pointedly that she wouldn't want him back, and give her someone to hate.' There was so much left unsaid, but what was the point of telling of Colin's threats when they had come to nothing, or of his reputation, when that would only make her father fret that he had let her down. 'I only knew I couldn't let the marriage go ahead.' There was no need to say there wouldn't have been a marriage, either.

'So you saved Felicity's pride at the expense of your reputation. You had to love her very much to do that. I'm ashamed to think it was my own stubbornness which added to the hurt,' Sir John confessed, then looked at his eldest daughter with a frown. 'But if you didn't love him, why did you marry him?'

Maxi had long ago decided what answer she would give if she was ever asked. She licked her lips, never finding it easy to lie to her family. 'He managed to persuade me that it would work, and I guess I was so angry when nobody would believe me that I thought it didn't matter that I didn't love him. When it didn't work, I got a divorce.' It sounded plausible, and there was no reason why anyone should disbelieve her after so long. Only a few people knew the truth of her marriage, and the memories she refused to resurrect. 'It's all water under the bridge.'

After a pause, her father sighed, holding out his hand, and she rose fluidly to take it. 'If you can forgive an old man, Maxine, it would make him very happy. It seems we've all made mistakes, but if you've managed to put yours behind you then perhaps I'll forgive myself. Have you told your mother?'

Feeling quite misty with tears, Maxi quickly bent and kissed his weathered cheek. 'Of course I forgive you, and no, I haven't told Mother. Perhaps you could, but I'd rather tell Fliss myself, if you don't mind. When she's more receptive.'

'Of course, my dear. Now, off you go and join the party again before you're missed.' He shooed her away, only to halt her at the door. 'And Maxine ... welcome home.'

Maxi hugged that belated greeting to her. With her father's acceptance, a weight had been lifted from her shoulders. Lighter of heart and spirit, she headed back to the party, and had no sooner walked in than Andy claimed her for a dance. In high spirits, he flirted with her, and knowing it meant nothing, she teased him back. Until, over his shoulder, she caught sight of her sister's mutinous face. The storm signals were well and truly out.

She wisely refused a second dance, although she found herself getting more and more irritated with Fliss's behaviour. She wasn't short of partners after that; however, she was shortly to discover that ignoring threatening storm clouds was a dangerous thing. An hour or so later, while she was taking a breather with some old acquaintances, strong fingers suddenly clamped hold of her wrist. Glancing round, she fully expected to see Kerr, but found instead a far from cheerful Andy at her side. In fact he looked positively grim with anger.

'Dance with me,' he said abruptly, and Maxi had little choice but to acquiesce as he nearly dragged her away.

'Andy? What on earth's the matter?' she queried, twisting her head to see if she could spot her sister, but for once Fliss was nowhere in sight.

Seeing her actions, Andy uttered a hoarse laugh. 'You won't find her. We had a row and she flung off in a huff.'

Maxi stared at him in consternation. 'Oh, no!' she exclaimed, with ready sympathy, then a far from welcome thought flashed through her mind and her eyes narrowed suspiciously. 'Was it about me?' she demanded tersely.

His snort was eloquent. 'Who else? You're all she ever talks about these days! Can you believe it? First she accuses me of having an affair with you, and then, when I do manage to calm her down, she orders me not to dance with you, or even talk to you, to prove I'm not!' he exclaimed in a furious undertone.

Maxi closed her eyes, counted to ten and then forced herself not to give in to temptation and let fly. 'Andy, you've got to go and find her this instant!' she ordered swiftly, seeing the awful implications looming over her head.

But Andy could be as bullish as his brother in some things. 'No way. If I see her now, I'd strangle her. If she doesn't trust me, then to hell with her!'

Maxi ground her teeth in exasperation. Why was it that whenever Fliss had a fight it was herself who ended up bearing the brunt of it? OK, she could see he was hurt, but two wrongs had never made a right yet. Keeping a weather eye out for her own personal nemesis, she gave him a shake. 'This isn't the way, Andy, believe me. What you need to do is find Fliss, sit down and talk about it.' Unfortunately it was like applying logic to a mule. And then the situation worsened rapidly when out of the corner of her eye she caught sight of her sister's white face. 'Andy! Stop this! Oh, you idiot, trying to make her jealous just won't work!'

Far from helping, matters suddenly went from worse to diabolical, for Andy had seen Fliss too, and instead of releasing Maxi, he chose to sweep her closer in a gesture of defiance that was like setting off a time bomb. That was when another factor entered the lists. All around eyes were watching them avidly, and the whispering was almost audible above the music. Maxi had a dreadful presentiment.

'Andy, where were you when you argued?' she gritted through her teeth.

He laughed hollowly. 'In the lounge. It caused quite a scene.'

'Oh, God!' Now she understood. It was almost exactly like before, only this time everyone would believe the worst without any foundation. She felt herself go white with anger. How could Andy have done this to her? How dared he use her? He might well be angry and upset, but that was no excuse, no excuse at all.

There was so much strength in her attempt to pull away that Andy was startled into letting her go. Nor did she stop there, but gave him a resounding slap on his cheek before pushing her way through the now openly gawking crowd and out on to the terrace. She had no idea where she was going from there, but the owner of the steely fingers which clamped about her arm had no doubts, steering her purposefully over the grass towards the ghost-like structure of the summer-house. Only when she had been pushed inside was she released, and had she been in any doubt who she would see when she turned round the hairs on the back of her neck would have told her.

Even in the gloom she recognised Kerr's large figure blocking the exit. 'Still protecting little brother, are we?' she drawled nastily, so angry she had to take it out on someone.

There was a strange note in his voice as it came to her across the wooden building. 'I thought I was, but now I'm not sure what the hell was going on.'

Her laugh held a disturbing note of hysteria. 'You must be the only one who doesn't!'

'Then enlighten me,' he invited grimly, pacing a step or two closer.

Maxi held up her hand to keep him at bay. 'Stay right where you are. Come any closer and I'm likely to kill you as well as your brother!' she ranted murderously.

'Very interesting, but I'm just as much in the dark as I ever was. Why don't you start at the beginning?' Kerr suggested, pressing her down into the nearest seat and holding her there firmly when she seemed inclined to rebel.

Maxi shrugged him off as her temper began to subside. 'I don't know the beginning! All I could get out of Andy is that the pair of them had a row—over me, naturally—and the next thing I know, he's using me to make her jealous!'

'Ah!'

'Don't use that tone of voice with me!' she shot back testily, and could almost see his eyebrows go up. 'Your brother is a double-dealing rat!'

'I'll agree he isn't functioning too well at the moment,' Kerr agreed thoughtfully.

Her navy eyes burned with dislike. 'Now everyone thinks the worst, not just Fliss. That should make you ecstatic!'

There was definite amusement in his tone of voice. 'I'll agree it was a fortuitous move. I couldn't have planned it better.'

'Don't imagine you've won. Fliss saw me slap him!' she countered.

'Of course, but everyone knows a slap at the right time is more of a come-on than a deterrent.'

Maxi winced, knowing he was right, and feeling his trap closing even more tightly around her. 'I'm not getting involved with you, Kerr. I don't like you,' she bit out, although she felt powerless, because they both knew now she must agree in the end.

'I don't like you either, but I'm willing to put up with you for the sake of a good cause,' he drawled sardonically, making her wince again.

Abruptly she shot to her feet. 'Don't profess to anything so noble as caring! We both know why you're doing this, and Fliss and Andy are just an excuse!'

There was steel in his voice. 'Don't imagine I don't care, because I do.'

She gritted her teeth. 'You've a grudge you want settled, and you've no compunction about killing two birds with one stone!' Her hand slapped helplessly against her thigh. 'Why now?'

He came up behind her. 'Because I made myself a promise, and I always make a point of keeping them.'

Maxi kept her back to him, but she was so aware of him that her skin prickled. Knowing she had to keep him at a distance somehow, she used the only weapon she had. 'I want you to know that although I'm forced into agreeing to this, I despise you.'

His laugh rang with triumph. 'I wouldn't have it any other way.'

God, how she hated him. 'Don't crow too soon. You know I'll never be convincing.'

At that two warm, strong hands moulded her shoulders. 'Oh, but you will. You won't even have to grit your teeth and bear it.' His voice had dropped an octave, becoming low and husky, and his thumbs began describing lazy circles below her nape.

Suddenly plunged into a maelstrom of sensation, Maxi closed her eyes in an effort to retain control, but that only made it worse. Her brain told her to move, but no part of her could obey. Her skin burned where he touched her, and her breathing was going haywire. Only once in her life before had she felt like this, longing to take one step back which would bring her up against his strong, solid flesh. Then, to her shame, she realised she had done that very thing, because when he spoke, there was satisfaction in his tone.

'You see how easy it is when you stop fighting yourself? This is all you have to do to make Fliss happy, and what makes Fliss happy makes Andy happy.'

Her throat was tight with violent emotions. Unable to move, she felt as if she had betrayed herself. Had Trilby felt like this when Svengali put her under his spell? Had she felt torn, too? Wanting to go, wanting to stay. She groaned silently. She had come home to find peace of mind, not this torment of the senses.

She could have wept for lost dreams. 'And will this make you happy too? To have me dancing to your tune?'

His lips brushed her ear, sending a shiver through the length of her. 'As I'm paying the piper, yes. But never mind, darling, there's still a pot of gold at the end of the rainbow. When I think you've danced enough, you and I can wave goodbye and go our separate ways, never to meet again.'

That moment couldn't come soon enough for her, and she finally found the strength to step away, causing his hands to fall to his sides. 'And if I fail?' she queried, grateful that her voice sounded strong. Indeed, her thought processes were slowly returning to normal now that she had put some distance between them.

Kerr came and stood beside her in the doorway. 'You won't, I'm sure. This isn't the game you played when you took Ellis from Fliss. Then you made everyone believe you were hot for him, but with us there won't be any need for pretence. You respond to me and we both know it. You'll make it look convincing because you won't be able to help yourself.'

For a moment she didn't speak, because she simply couldn't. The truth of what he said chilled her to the bone. The potency of Kerr's attraction dissolved her defences as if they didn't exist. With his hands two points of warmth on her flesh, she had wanted him to touch her. Wanted him to kiss her the way he had that morning. That was why she was scared. Because he could tempt her along paths that must lead nowhere.

He believed she had played a game with Colin, that she had enjoyed it. She almost laughed. It had been as much fun as having a tooth pulled without benefit of anaesthetic. For Colin she had acted her socks off, in ways Kerr would never imagine. But she had sworn never again, and kept to it. When her marriage had ended, she had adopted a celibate lifestyle without any regret. She had dated since, but no man had ever tempted her to break her own rules, or come close to making her think she could trust them or put her happiness in their hands. But Kerr was different. He had the power to tempt her, pure and simple. In that lay the greatest danger of all, because if he knew it the man he was now would use that knowledge against her.

It became imperative to lay down the ground rules. 'I'll do only what I have to do to convince Fliss, but no more. Whatever you think of me, Kerr, I don't sleep around, and I don't intend to break that rule just for you,' she told him flatly.

'Although I doubt if I'd have much trouble changing your mind, you should wait until you're asked. As it happens, I have some rules of my own, and I'm choosy about who shares my bed,' he retorted pithily.

It wasn't very complimentary, but she was relieved none the less. 'Just make sure it stays that way.'

'Or you'll what? Don't start ordering me about, darling, because that's the safest way of getting me to prove my point,' Kerr informed her bluntly.

She shivered but refused to cower. 'If you've finished throwing your weight around, we should go before they come looking for us.'

'Keep sticking your chin out that way, and you're bound to get it clipped,' Kerr remarked curtly. Slipping an arm around her waist as they descended the steps to the lawn, he immediately felt her tense and try to pull away. 'If you're going to do that every time I touch you, we might as well give up right now!' he hissed close to her ear.

Maxi shot him a baleful look. 'If you wanted an actress, you've picked the wrong woman!' she snapped back.

'Stop pretending to be a shrinking violet. With your track record it's hardly believable,' he jeered in a violent undertone.

That was one goad too many, and with scarcely a moment's hesitation, she brought her heel down hard on his instep, and gained grim satisfaction from hearing his grunt of pain. 'If you don't stop insulting me, Kerr, I'll aim for an even more vulnerable spot!'

In reply he unleashed a broadside which left her grinding her teeth silently, because they were approaching the house, giving her no time to respond. 'Try it, and you'll be flat on your back in a second. Or is that what you're hoping for?'

Stopping just on the edge of the area the house illuminated, he urged her to face him, slipping his other arm around her. 'We have an audience, and, if I'm not mistaken, our young lovebirds are part of it. Let's not disappoint them.'

Navy eyes glittered angrily. Her hands came up to his chest, halting his descending head. 'My God, but you're enjoying this, aren't you?' she seethed, and instantly felt his arms tighten about her.

'You're damn right! Now kiss me, Maxi,' he ordered mockingly, then took her lips with a mastery that was designed to shock and thrill, and did both with devastating effect. There was no time to think as, with explicit sensuality, his tongue explored her mouth, instantly arousing a need to meet and match it. His grunt of triumph told her that she had, and with a despairing sense of inevitability she pressed closer, losing herself in a kiss that tortured her senses, creating a need that no one kiss could satisfy.

That first kiss became two, and suddenly they were clinging, swaying as if in a strong breeze as their bodies strained closer. Kerr's hand came up to fix in her hair, holding her so that he could ravage her senses at will, and for one delirious moment the world went spinning off its axis. Then, just as abruptly, it was over. The alchemy of his lips was removed. Oh, God, Maxi groaned silently, gripping his shoulders because her legs trembled so. It was worse than she had expected.

'"You have witchcraft in your lips",' he quoted huskily, and with a jolt she recognised the words from the love scene in *Henry V*. She couldn't help but look up, only to find his eyes filled with a blatant mockery. Hurt more than it had seemed possible to be, she glanced down, and above her head Kerr gave a slow laugh.

'That should certainly give them something to think about.'

Maxi struggled to free herself of the morass of her senses. Calling herself a fool for allowing herself to be drawn in so neatly, she knew it was desperately important to sound as cool as he did. 'I'm so glad I came up to expectation,' she managed to drawl, and found herself staring into gleaming grey eyes.

'Oh, you did more than that and you know it,' he responded drily. 'You certainly know how to make a man want you, don't you, Maxi? I hope you're not thinking of playing your tricks with me.'

His words cooled the fever in her blood. 'I wouldn't dream of it. I value my sanity too much! Don't you dare blame me for your libido. If you want a woman, go and find one—don't look at me!'

He released her instantly, but his eyes sent a warning that made her shiver. 'Don't say another word, if you value more than just your sanity!'

His response was a surprise revelation, and she knew she must have hit him on the raw because he would never have given even that little away under other circumstances. So, she hadn't imagined that compulsion when he kissed her, although he had tried quite cleverly to hide it. Having scored a surprise hit, Maxi found a perverse pleasure in slipping her hand through his arm, urging him forward. 'Poor Kerr, you didn't count on being turned on yourself, did you? But never mind, it will just make it all so much more believable!' If anything could give her pleasure, then it was knowing that they found themselves in the same boat. He didn't like being attracted any more than she did.

'Put a curb on that tongue of yours, darling,' he advised, caustically. 'You don't want the kind of trouble I could bring you. Now, if you could just manage to look as if the kiss didn't leave you with a bad taste in your mouth, we're laughing.'

She dredged up one of her famous smiles, pleased that at least one of her darts had found a mark. It gave her something to aim for. 'I'll do my best, but you aren't the easiest person to think pleasant thoughts of,' she enlarged with a world-weary sigh.

Having reached the doorway to the room where the dancing had continued unabated, Kerr turned to gaze down at her. His smile was tender, but his grey eyes chilled her. 'Then think of something that does, darling.

I don't care if it's ice-cream. Let's dance. It will keep my hands busy, and well away from your throat!' he hissed out of the corner of his mouth.

Maxi let out a gurgling laugh of real amusement, allowing him to lead her into the mêlée and hold her close. There were chinks in his armour that she couldn't resist probing, even though she knew it was wiser to keep him at a distance. 'I just love it when you say those sexy things to me!' she teased dangerously, then gasped as his teeth came down sharply on her earlobe.

'Cat!'

. 'Rat!' she snapped back, and experienced a delicious shiver as he laughed huskily.

'Sheathe your claws, darling, before I declaw you.'

That brought back memories which dulled her eyes just as if someone had flicked a switch. 'You're too late, that was done a long time ago,' she stated leadenly, and instantly regretted the admission when he eased away enough to look down at her.

'Somebody else not like the way you play your games, Maxi?' he taunted softly.

'Actually he was a games master himself, *par excellence*.'

Two expressive eyebrows rose. 'The biter bit? Now there's a novelty. I'd like to meet the man.'

She shook her head emphatically. 'Take it from me, you wouldn't.' Colin, she had discovered to her cost, had had a capacity for evil with untapped depths.

'Afraid I might pick up some tips?'

Recovering her poise, she let her eyes drift away over his shoulder. 'You're doing fine by yourself. You don't need any help,' she replied drily, then through the mass of moving bodies she caught sight of a familiar one, and caught her breath. 'We're being watched.'

Kerr's response was to draw her close again. 'It has to be Fliss, Andy's over by the door. How does she look?'

Carefully Maxi took another look. 'Shocked.'

'Well, at least she hasn't run away in tears! How much do you bet she now decides to give me a few well chosen words of wisdom?' Kerr drawled in amusement.

Unseen, Maxi grinned. There spoke the voice of experience. 'I don't bet,' she said crushingly, not wanting to find any more reasons to like him.

'You surprise me, I would have thought gambling was just your cup of tea. However, I'll tell you what we'll do. We'll have lunch together tomorrow, and if I'm right you'll pay,' he proposed easily.

Maxi tensed again. 'Lunch? Do we have to?'

'You surely didn't think one kiss and a dance would suffice?' Kerr challenged scornfully, and she winced.

She could hope, couldn't she? 'I suppose that means dinner, too?'

The music changed to a faster beat, and she didn't protest when Kerr led her from the floor and into the other room where the buffet had been set up. 'Now you're getting the picture. You could look on it as your engagement gift to Fliss—giving her back her peace of mind.' Slowly he began to fill two plates.

But at the cost of her own, Maxi thought despairingly. She had always known this visit wasn't going to be easy, but not just how complicated it could turn out to be. 'I thought of getting her a vase,' she said whimsically.

He looked down at her with a grin. 'Believe me, this will be much more appreciated. Not thinking of chickening out, are you?' Handing her a plate piled with food, he took a forkful from his own and held it to her lips. 'Here, try this.'

'Thanks, but I've been feeding myself since I was two years old,' she refused sarcastically.

Kerr didn't lower the fork. 'Clever girl, but this is much more romantic. I thought you would have known that, or have your encounters with men been too... involved to encompass food?'

What she wouldn't give to be able to slap him! Instead, eyes flashing fire, she parted her lips and accepted the offering. Only Kerr heard the snap of her teeth on the fork.

Something flared at the back of his eyes. 'I think I've just avoided losing an arm. Or was it my throat you were imagining those pearly teeth closing on?'

'Now, what do you think?' she asked sweetly, keeping the smile pinned to her face. For a moment she concentrated on eating, although she wasn't really hungry. 'I suppose you've thought of how we're to get ourselves out of this once Fliss has been convinced?'

'The simplest thing would be to let them think the affair has died a natural death. It shouldn't be hard, with me here and you in London,' Kerr outlined sensibly. 'Or would your ego demand that you break it off?'

Maxi drew in an angry breath. If he kept making cracks like that, she'd be driven to doing something drastic. 'Fortunately my ego isn't so fragile. But I'll give you the same opportunity, if you like.'

He declined her offer with a shake of his head. 'I'll pass.'

Maxi shot him a mocking look. 'Playing the gentleman.'

'I was raised to be one,' Kerr acknowledged.

'I don't think it was very gentlemanly to kiss a woman as a punishment,' she rejoined swiftly, only to see him smile.

'Does that still smart?'

Damn, it was so aggravating to find him so attractive when he laughed. It undermined her resolve not to let him get to her. 'An apology would be nice. But I suppose that would be asking too much?'

'You suppose correctly,' Kerr said smoothly.

'Then you're no gentleman at all,' she replied scornfully.

'There are times when it doesn't pay to be. On the other hand, if you were honest, you'd admit a woman doesn't always want a man to be a gentleman,' he added suggestively, shooting her a curious look. 'Or do you expect your lover to say "please" when he's in your bed, rather than just please you?'

It was an idle question, and he had no way of knowing what a hornet's nest he had stirred up inside her. If by lover he meant someone you went to bed with, then it should be singular, but if he meant someone who took you to bed and gave you pleasure, then she hadn't even had one. Glancing down, she found she had a death grip on her fork, and hastily set it and the plate aside.

'Well,' she managed to say with admirable calmness, 'that's something you're never likely to find out!'

Grey eyes gleamed. 'Is that a challenge? If so, I ought to warn you, I very rarely ignore them.'

'There are exceptions to every rule. I'd advise you to make me one.'

'Now you're making me curious,' he declared.

'Curiosity killed the cat.'

'So they say, but perhaps what he found out beforehand made the end worthwhile. It's a tempting thought. After all, I'd be lying if I didn't admit I found the thought of making love to you arousing. You're beautiful, the kind of woman men fantasise about, and I'm only human,' he confessed in a voice carefully lowered to reach only her ears.

'I can think of a more accurate description, and, that being the case, you can keep your fantasies to yourself,' she strictured disdainfully, and might have guessed it would only draw forth yet another mocking reply.

'Not even the slightest bit curious, Maxi? Hasn't it crossed your mind just once to wonder what it would have been like to make love with me?'

Her eyes flashed navy sparks of derision. 'Not once! Not even a passing thought! Not even that much!' She clicked her fingers under his nose. Lord, his ego needed pricking badly. Not that she had lied. To think of what might have been in the midst of a painful reality was a road leading to madness.

His brow creased. 'Now, do I believe you or not? Somehow it just doesn't have the ring of truth. All those years, and not even a momentary speculation.'

She could take a lot, her marriage had proved that, but there were limits. It didn't matter that he didn't know he was probing a wound that still went deep. When she was hurting, her instinct was to hurt back. 'All right, I'll tell you. Yes, I thought about it, and then I dismissed it. I dismissed it because you were nothing to me and never could be, and there were plenty of fish in the sea. Like you, I'm human, and that means I make mistakes. You were one. But I've made it a policy never to make the same mistakes again.'

When she came to a breathless halt, she realised she had succeeded beyond her wildest dreams. He wasn't just angry, he was coldly furious.

'Never?' he taunted chillingly. 'You know, I'm beginning to think it might just be worth breaking my own rules to prove you wrong,' he declared tautly. Taking her hand in a painfully tight grip, he drew it through his arms. 'Let's circulate. We've monopolised each other for just about as long as I can stand.'

Thoughts in a chaotic turmoil, she allowed him to lead her away. Nobody would know that behind her bright smile she was asking herself what on earth she had just done.

# CHAPTER SIX

NEXT morning Maxi came awake with a groan. Something had stirred her but she couldn't say what. Coming up on her elbow, she swept her hair out of her eyes and stared blearily at the clock. Blinking, she did a double-take, not believing it had said six-thirty the first time. Collapsing back on the pillows with a heartfelt groan, she jack-knifed into a sitting position when a voice spoke next to her ear.

'A cup of tea will wake you up, but personally I think the bleary look will be a better effect.'

Jaw down by her ankles, Maxi stared dumbfounded at Kerr, who sat propped up against her headboard, dressed in a knee-length robe and, she had no doubt, nothing else, carefully preserving a cup of tea from spilling. Unaware of just how alluring she looked in a nightdress which had slipped from one shoulder, and with her hair rumpled, she scrambled from the bed, chest rising and falling rapidly in mounting anger.

'What the hell do you think you're doing?'

Eyes aglow as he inspected her charms, Kerr raised a hand. 'Shush! Keep your voice down. There's no need to cry rape. I'm merely adding verisimilitude to the idea that you and I are a hot number,' he explained, crossing his legs and revealing altogether too much thigh.

Maxi instantly felt her stomach lurch in response, and hastily averted her eyes from the sexy picture he made, even if he did need a shave. It was hard to concentrate when the sight of him made her insides melt, and the words spluttered out.

'I don't care what you're doing, you aren't doing it here! Get out!' A slightly trembling finger pointed to the door. 'I mean it, Kerr, get out, right now!' she ordered, then got caught on the end of a dazzling grey gaze.

'Make me,' he challenged softly, setting his cup aside and crossing his arms, waiting.

If he thought she wouldn't, he was much mistaken. She was angry enough to toss him across the room. With the growl of a fighting tigress, she rounded the bed in less than a second and caught his arm, tugging for all she was worth. Just for a moment she thought she was succeeding, but only because Kerr was moving too. Swinging his legs off the bed, he used her momentary imbalance to jerk her forward, twisting her neatly on to the bed and rolling over to pin her there.

It had happened so fast that she hadn't been able to resist, but even as her heart skipped a beat she was opening her lips to scream. All that emitted was a strangled moan as his lips came down on hers, plundering her mouth with a sensuality which sent her senses swimming dizzily. The hands she had locked in his hair to thrust him away, clung on instead as her body played her traitor. Her nightdress had risen, and she could feel the pleasurable roughness of his thigh between hers. With a silent groan she fought the longing to rub herself against him, and was almost at the point of losing that battle too when he suddenly pushed himself away from her and sat up.

Gathering scattered wits, she saw him glance at the clock, and at the same time heard a door open further along the corridor.

'Six forty-five. Fliss certainly is a punctual girl,' Kerr observed, standing and looking down at her still lying sprawled on the bed. 'Like that you look as if you've spent a glorious night of debauchery. I think she'll get the message.' With a last slow look, he turned and headed for the door.

She understood then what that meant, what his whole presence had been about, and shamed colour swept into her cheeks as she recalled she was still lying there so suggestively. Struggling upright, angry tears making her eyes glitter at the way he had used her, she stumbled over his slippers. Kerr was already going through the door as she picked them up and ran after him.

'Don't forget these, you rat!' she cried, lobbing them after him. One caught him on the back and made him turn, revealing a face alight with mocking laughter.

'Quiet, darling, we don't want the whole house to know. Morning, Fliss.' This last was addressed to her sister, who had come to a stunned halt only a yard away.

Maxi had been so intent on Kerr that she hadn't seen they weren't alone. It didn't take much intelligence to put a telling interpretation on the scene, and one look at Fliss showed the message had been received. It was hard to know which of the two sisters was more embarrassed, but Maxi didn't wait to find out; she dived back into her room and slammed the door behind her.

'Oh, God!' Pressing her hands to her cheeks, she wished the floor would open and swallow her up. Then almost at once she straightened. Why the hell should she feel cheap? It was all Kerr's fault. He had had no right to set her up that way. It was one thing to agree to put Fliss's mind at rest, but quite another to make herself look easy!

With her dislike growing by leaps and bounds, Maxi went into the bathroom, determined to wash away every last touch of him. She emerged cleaner and more level-headed. Of course he hadn't had to use the method he had. The choice had been deliberate, to pay her back for what she had said last night. He was totally without scruples, so why should she be so nice? It was time to take the gloves off.

Her hackles up, she dressed in a buttercup-yellow halter-necked sun dress, put matching canvas espadrilles on her feet, brushed her hair until it shone, and went down to breakfast. Prepared to do battle, she was just crossing the hall when the telephone rang, and she automatically answered it.

'Maxi?' Andy's question came out hesitantly.

'Hello, Andy. Did you want to speak to Fliss?' She kept her voice cool, not quite sure if she'd forgiven him yet. Especially when, despite their argument, he and Fliss had ended the evening together happily enough.

'Actually, it was you I wanted to talk to,' he corrected awkwardly. 'I wanted to apologise for my stupid behaviour last night. Even if Fliss did make me angry, I had no business using you to make a point. I'm sorry. I fully deserved that slap. Do you forgive me?'

He sounded so boyish and contrite, she didn't have the heart to deny him. 'How could I refuse such a gracious apology. You're forgiven.'

'Great. Now I don't have to worry about Kerr coming after me for stepping on his toes! I had no idea you and he were getting on so well,' he declared facetiously. 'I can't imagine how Fliss managed to get such a bee in her bonnet about you and me, when it's as plain as the nose on your face where your interest lies.'

Maxi was glad he couldn't see the colour rise in her cheeks as she wondered just how much he knew. She fiddled with her hair. 'Er—it was that obvious, was it?'

Andy chuckled. 'Getting clearer by the hour by the sound of it,' he enlarged, making her heart sink. 'Boy, won't I pull Kerr's leg about this. You know, I always thought he had a soft spot for you, even when he was running you down over that Ellis chap. I'm glad he seems to have changed his mind.'

Maxi was hardly in a position to argue the point, even though she could give him chapter and verse about how wrong he was. 'So am I, Andy,' she concurred wryly, keeping up the fiction. 'Do you want me to get Fliss now?'

'She always rings me before breakfast, but thanks all the same,' he refused, and a short while later they rang off.

And that, Maxi thought glumly, explained exactly how much he did know. Fliss hadn't been able to keep the scene she had witnessed to herself. Just how many others she had told didn't bear thinking about. Deciding breakfast would sit like lead in her stomach, she continued on her way out to the terrace.

Last night she had actually started to think things were looking up. Her mother had come to her room after everyone had gone to bed, and they had had a long chat. Her father had been as good as his word, and now a great deal of misunderstanding had been put right. They had both cried a lot, but it had cleared the air. She had gone to sleep believing that if only Fliss would relax hostilities enough to listen for a change then her visit would be a complete success.

There was, however, still one fly in the ointment. A bluebottle named Kerr. After his behaviour this morning, she felt even less inclined to give him an explanation. As for having a soft spot for her, Andy was mistaken. He didn't miss an opportunity to get in a dig. But that wasn't what really worried her. She could take the animosity, and give back almost as good as she got. The danger lay in their physical attraction. He might not be the Harlequin she remembered, but the effect he had on her hadn't changed. Her defences against him were puny, so, if he really did make a play for her, could she resist him?

Stupid, there was no 'could' about it. She had to. That was the legacy of her marriage to Colin. It had been a battleground, and she had won the hard way. Because he hadn't been able to have her, he had wanted to destroy her. She wouldn't let any man try to do that to her again, however much he attracted her. Kerr had the power to sweep everything from her mind with just one kiss, and Kerr wanted revenge. Oh, he hadn't said 'destroy', but if he used her attraction against her that would surely be the result, because 'love', 'marriage' and 'forever' were not words in his vocabulary. She had to get control over her wayward senses, because control was all she had to save her pride with.

Lost deep in her troubled thoughts, she didn't realise she was no longer alone until the grate of iron on cement broke through, making her jump. Glancing round, she discovered Fliss had come to join her. Like herself, her sister looked cool in a strappy sundress covered in sunflowers.

'What are you and Kerr up to?' was Fliss's opening gambit, stunning Maxi, who hadn't been prepared for any doubt after that scene earlier.

'Up to?' she laughed huskily, prepared to follow a course not of her choosing because she had no option. 'I thought it was obvious, or do you really need me to spell it out, Fliss?' She gave her sister an old-fashioned look.

Colour stole into her sister's cheek. 'But . . . after what you did, how could he?'

Maxi crossed her arms to better resist the temptation to give vent to her irritation, and shake some sense into her sibling. 'Perhaps he feels seven years is long enough to hold a grudge. Perhaps what he feels is stronger than an old prejudice. And what does it matter to you what Kerr does? I thought it was Andy you loved.'

Fliss shot to her feet. 'I do love Andy!'

'You'd never know it, the way you've been behaving. You're going the right way to losing him with your paranoia about me. I don't want Andy. I'm not a threat. If Kerr and I can be happy together, would you really begrudge us that?' It was stunning how easily one lie followed another.

Fliss flung her hands over her ears. 'Oh, I don't know what to think any more. Andy was so angry last night. I'd never seen him like that before. It frightened me. I don't want to lose him.'

Immediately Maxi's compassion rose to the fore and she crossed swiftly to her sister's side, slipping an arm around her. 'You won't, I promise. He loves you, he just doesn't understand why you're letting my visit affect you when he knows I don't want him. Everybody knows it but you.'

Fliss looked driven. 'You took Colin.'

Maxi sighed; would they always go round in circles like this? 'I know, but I can explain, if only you'd listen. I want us to be friends again, Fliss.'

Biting her lip, Fliss eased away. Finally she sent Maxi a sideways look. 'It's really Kerr you want?'

Oh, what a tangled web they were weaving. 'After catching us out this morning, I wouldn't have thought you could doubt it!' she said drily, and was more than a little amused to see Fliss regard her curiously.

'I don't know why. Oh, he's kind, I know, but much too bossy. Much too...you know,' she ended, with an expressive shiver.

Maxi had to laugh, for she certainly did know, and it was what attracted her. '*Vive la difference*,' she misused the quote, pleased to see her sister smile for a change.

'Well, well!' A voice from slightly below made them both start and turn towards the garden. 'It's good to see you two laughing,' Kerr declared, smiling up at them. Then holding out a peremptory hand to Maxi, he added,

'Come and say good morning, sweetheart, before it's afternoon.'

'I thought you'd already done that,' Fliss whispered archly, giggling, watching them with open interest.

Maxi, who could have done without the audience so that she could give him a piece of her mind, knew she had to respond or waste all the effort she had just gone to to reassure her sister. However, she didn't have to make it easy for him to gloat.

Crossing her arms, she tossed her head. 'I don't know that I want to. I'm not speaking to you.'

Kerr laughed up at her, and she could tell he wasn't pretending to enjoy himself. 'Don't tell me you were embarrassed because we got caught out? There's no need. Fliss is a woman of the world. She's engaged herself, so she understands these things. Come on, you know you want to,' he teased, and there was nothing else for her to do but descend the steps to where he stood.

He held open his arms. Dear God, he's too damned good at this, she thought as she went into them, feeling her heart contract as they closed about her. To counteract it, her eyes sent him a message of dislike, then his head dipped, and for the next few exhilarating seconds she couldn't have cared who was watching as Kerr wove his magic.

She tried later. Fought herself as hard as she could, but it was impossible not to press closer, to slide her hands up around his neck and let her fingers tangle in the vibrant mass of his hair. The touch and taste of him set off fireworks throughout her system. Though she knew she was only storing up grief for herself, there was just no way of denying him a response.

Her lips parted on a soundless sigh, welcoming the possessive thrust of his tongue, her own darting out to tease him until he pulled away, burying his lips against the throbbing pulse at the base of her throat. Then, as he began to explore lower, she heard from a distance the rapid departure of footsteps.

That brought with it a small measure of sanity, and her fingers tugged at his hair. 'She's gone,' she declared, then caught her breath as a shiver ran through her.

'Good,' Kerr muttered thickly, his breath brushing the inviting V of her breasts. 'Let's go to the summer-house.'

Oh, God! Trembling faintly in every limb, she closed her eyes and willed her blood to cool. 'Stop!' The command was almost a groan.

He finally raised his head, revealing banked fires in his eyes. 'Why? You don't really want me to.'

She tried to push herself to arm's length, but he defeated her easily. 'I do.'

'Liar,' he charged with a husky laugh, and brought his lips down on hers again. She struggled against drowning under the ravishment of his touch, feeling herself weakening. 'Maxine Ambro, you are some kind of witch,' he breathed against her lips, bringing her heart leaping into her throat.

It was the strength of desperation that helped her tear her lips free, but she could go no further. 'I'm just me, and I want you to let me go,' she ordered forcefully.

Breathing heavily, he stilled, regarding her through narrowed eyes. 'Is this some kind of game you play with all your lovers, or just me? I know you want me, Maxi, so why make me an exception? Or am I supposed to beg to be allowed into your bed?'

Maxi went white, unconscious of the pain revealed in her navy eyes. 'You really have the lowest possible opinion of me, don't you?'

Kerr's lips curled. 'Do you really expect me to see you as some kind of saint?' he drawled sardonically, making her gasp.

'I never said I was that, and you aren't either. I'm a human being, and I don't deserve to be talked to as if

I'm as cheap as dirt,' she threw back, lips tight with anger.

Kerr dragged a hand raggedly through his hair, his whole frame telling her he wasn't prepared to back down an inch. 'Don't expect an apology from me, Maxi. I've been angry with you too long for that. Maybe once I would have weakened before that hurt look in your eyes, but not now. Now I speak as I find. I want you, and I don't care to wait around in frustration while you play more of your little games, because I know you want me, too,' he growled.

Maxi hugged her arms around her waist. 'If you don't want to be frustrated, stay away from me, Kerr. I've already told you I won't get involved with you,' she reminded him curtly.

Throwing his head back, he uttered a mirthless laugh. 'How the hell do you think you're going to avoid it?'

Did he think she would just fall on her back if he clicked his fingers? Never! 'I'd go away.' Right now, this minute, she wanted to run, and run, and keep on running.

He didn't believe her. 'And leave Fliss in the lurch? I don't think so. For once in your life you're going to finish what you started. First Fliss, and then me. We never did settle what lay between us, and it's time we laid the ghost. Make no mistake, you will sleep with me, Maxi. Not because I demand it, but because it's what you want too. Every time I touch you I know that you're mine for the taking, but I won't have to take, because you'll give yourself to me.'

His words frightened her, not because of their intent, but because deep down inside she knew that every single one of them was true. Which made her denial all the more vehement. 'No!'

'Yes!' Kerr corrected emphatically. 'You're fooling yourself if you think this will just go away. It won't. One day or another, you're going to end up in my bed, and we both know it. Seven years is long enough to want someone. The ghosts need to be exorcised, and there's only one way to do it. I may have been surprised by how much I still want you, but that doesn't mean I can't control it, until you come to me. I won't force you, I won't need to, because you will come, that I promise you,' he finished grimly.

Throat working madly, she shook her head slowly, as if it hurt to move it. 'You're crazy if you think I'll stand for this!'

Kerr smiled thinly. 'What will you do, run? I don't think so. Your running days are over, as of now. It ends here. We'll end it together, the way it started.'

Hot tears stung the back of her eyes but she refused to let them fall. 'It will never be the way it was.'

His face became set. 'No. But better or worse, it's all we have. Now, as we have to spend time together, I suggest we try and get along. The car's waiting out front. If you're ready, we'll go to lunch. And don't tell me you're not hungry, because, the mood I'm in, the menu might well contain you!'

Shaking inwardly, Maxi promised to be outside in five minutes and escaped to her room. Once there, she sank weakly on to the dressing stool. Kerr's threat sat like a spear in her heart. It was cruel in its honesty, but what they felt was the darker side of the coin, passion without love or respect. She couldn't succumb to it, she had to fight, because she had sworn to herself that she would never give any man power over her unless he loved her as much as she loved him.

Three impatient blasts on a car horn brought her to her feet. He might summon, but she didn't have to respond. He had just told her himself that he would wait, but as far as she was concerned he would wait forever. She wasn't weak or a pushover, that she had proved a long time ago. She was more than a match for any man, as he was going to discover! Quickly running a brush through her hair, she grabbed up her bag and went to join him.

Kerr drove them to an inn several miles away. Nestled in a valley, the gardens ran down to the edge of a tumbling stream. It was pretty nearly idyllic, which was probably why there were plenty of customers, despite its being off the beaten track. The setting revitalised Maxi's appetite, reminding her she hadn't eaten so far today, and she readily agreed to Kerr's choice of a ploughman's lunch.

They ate outside in the sunshine, washing the food down with glasses of cider. Much to Maxi's relief, the drive seemed to have eased Kerr's mood, and the good food, plus the lazy warmth of the day, added to the mellowing process. Resting her elbows on the wooden table, and her chin in her hands, she studied him. In faded jeans and shirt, he couldn't look less like a lawyer. He could have been anybody, although the air he had about him made him quite definitely somebody. She experienced a wistfulness for things lost, then told herself not to be such a fool. It was a dangerous madness to imagine her stranger wouldn't have turned out like the Kerr she knew today. Love was blind, everybody knew that.

'Why did you choose the law? Because of your father?' she queried, breaking the mood of introspection, and bringing his eyes back from their study of a little girl playing catch with her doting father.

'No, although he likes to think so.' Kerr grinned affectionately at a memory. 'Nor was I a fan of Perry Mason. I chose law because I wanted to see justice done. I wanted to put wrong things right.'

She looked at him from under her lashes. Now that she could believe. 'And doubtless you thought you were

the best person to do it?' she murmured, lacing her words
with heavy irony.

He quirked a mocking eyebrow back at her and
laughed. 'Why not come right out and say it? I thought
I was the *only* person who could do it.'

Briefly she closed her eyes, cursing the diabolical fate
which could imbue your enemy with a heart-stopping
charm, while all other men became bland by com-
parison. 'I was giving you the benefit of modesty! So,
do you—put things right, I mean?'

'Wherever possible.'

Maxi studied him soberly. 'I think you must do it well,
because if you didn't you would have given up a long
time ago,' she decided, making his brows lift.

A faint frown creased his brow. 'That's very per-
ceptive of you.'

She looked askance. 'Don't sound so surprised. I'm
not just a pretty face,' she said meaningfully.

Kerr sat up and faced her, mimicking her posture. 'No,
your body's pretty spectacular too.'

Maxi didn't laugh. 'I suppose I should have expected
that sort of sexist remark from you. To you a model is
probably some little bimbo with a pea for a brain, who
bed-hops her way to the top, isn't she?'

'I never said that, nor do I think so little of your profession to have even thought it,' he denied evenly, eyes
challenging her to argue.

'Perhaps not, but you'd find it easy to believe of me,
wouldn't you?'

He didn't deny it, merely asked, 'Does it matter what
I think?'

Though she knew it shouldn't, it did, and that was
crazy thinking. 'Not in the least.'

His eyes mocked her. 'Then it wouldn't interest you
to know I do think you're more than just a body? I've
watched you with your father's guests. You're thoughtful

and intelligent. You have the knack of putting people at their ease and making other women feel you aren't a threat to them. Moreover, you not only know when to speak, but when to say nothing at all. You're a good listener. Which makes me wonder,' he finished cryptically.

Maxi, who had nearly fallen off her seat at the unexpected praise he had heaped on her, struggled through a fog of warmth and confusion, and found her voice. 'Wonder what?'

'What made you choose modelling.'

Maxi was startled into pulling a rueful face. 'You may have noticed that I'm not short.'

Kerr didn't laugh, but his eyes danced. 'It hadn't escaped my notice.'

Her lashes fell quickly, as alarm shot through her at the way her heart had contracted. Why, oh, why, did she suddenly have to feel they were on the same wavelength? Only a couple of hours ago they had been at each other's throats. It made no sense. All it did was keep her off balance when she needed to be firm in her resolve. Clenching her fingers, she forced herself to remain cool.

'Well, when I left school I didn't know what I wanted to do. I knew I didn't want to study law, which was my father's wish. Nothing really appealed to me until I saw an advertisement for models. I didn't think I was too bad-looking, and the height was right, so I said, "Why not?" Unfortunately, my parents were horrified. Modelling was like white slavery to them. They vetoed the idea immediately.'

'Which only made you more determined to do it,' Kerr put in drily, and she sighed, remembering all the painful arguments.

'Exactly. I really wanted their approval, but I didn't need it because I was eighteen. Finally I ran away and did it anyway,' she confessed, and looked at him challengingly. 'Aren't you going to tell me I was wilful? That, having hurt my parents once, I was quite capable of doing it again?'

'Is that what you're telling me?' he countered smoothly.

Wondering why he had bypassed an opportunity to get in a dig, she shook her head. 'No. I knew it was what I really wanted to do, and that I could be a success. Which I am. End of story.'

'That's rather over-simplifying the case, surely. As the saying goes, many are called, few are chosen. You didn't get to the top of the tree without good hard work,' Kerr objected.

'And a slice of luck.'

'It's as useful in my profession as it is in yours. Go on.'

Maxi hesitated, because to go on would be to skate very near dangerous ground. On the other hand, she had never gone out of her way to avoid confrontation. She eyed him consideringly. 'Are you sure you want to hear this?' she cautioned.

'I take it this is "skeleton in the closet" time. Put it this way: if you don't tell me, you'll have me imagining all sorts of things. The truth can hardly be worse,' Kerr encouraged, with the sort of logic she was sure he found useful in his work.

She shrugged. 'All right, if you insist. Colin and I were married in the States, which isn't as important as the fact that I went back there to get my divorce. Anyway, as fortune had it I met a woman on an internal flight who was going west for the same reason. She just happened to be a New York agent. One thing led to another, and before I knew it I'd been chosen for a major campaign.' She hadn't looked back since.

'So you went on to fame and fortune. What happened to Ellis?'

That was a horse of another colour, and she let her eyes drop. 'I wouldn't know,' she said shortly. 'I haven't seen him in over six years.' Not since that last day in the courtroom, when he had looked at her with such venom. If she didn't see him for the next sixty years, she wouldn't be sorry.

Kerr toyed with his empty glass, not looking at her when he spoke. 'I've heard that companies insist the models used in their campaigns have squeaky-clean private lives,' he observed, and finally raised his head to spear her on the end of a grey glance.

She should have known the *bonhomie* wouldn't last, she thought, sitting back tensely. 'You heard correctly, and mine can stand any amount of inspection.'

Kerr raised his brows. 'Relax, I didn't mean to offend you.'

She eyed him askance. 'Not much.'

He laughed. 'I apologise most humbly,' he declared, in a tone which quite clearly said he wasn't sorry at all, and that he and humility were total strangers.

Stiffening, Maxi pursed her lips in annoyance. 'I see. Lunch is over. Now it's Round Two.'

She had amused him. 'Is that how you see us, as two boxers in the ring? Forever circling each other, looking for a way to get under the other's guard? Are you a dirty fighter, Maxi? You'll need to be if you expect to beat me.'

'I'm learning. After all, I have the best teacher,' she sniped, staring him out.

'*Touché*. However, I have no intention of coming to blows this afternoon. I'd planned on taking a walk along the river instead. You can stay here or join me if you wish.' Getting up, he rounded the table and helped her over the bench.

Maxi looked sceptical. 'Do I really have a choice?'

'No,' he confirmed, keeping a tight hold of her hand as he led the way down the river.

'That's what I thought,' she muttered, reluctantly amused. His conceit was incredible. But why should she be surprised? She'd never really known this man at all. She hated him with good reason, but there were times when he reminded her of a romantic stranger, and all she wanted to do was stop fighting. Like now, when the touch of his hand was sending tingles of pleasure up her arm.

'By the way, you owe me for the lunch. Fliss caught me at breakfast, and did her best to convince me to stop seeing you. She wasn't best pleased when I refused, and told me I was mad.'

Behind his back she pulled a face. It wasn't very flattering to hear your sister considered you some sort of *femme fatale*. Yet perhaps she wouldn't be thinking that for very much longer. Then, if she would only listen to the truth, they could be friends again. She wanted that very much.

Beyond that she didn't think, concentrating instead on the scenery. The path followed the contours of the river, deviating only round rocks and trees. It was beautifully soothing, and Maxi made no objection when, after half an hour, Kerr suggested they cross a stile and make their way to the top of the valley side. It was a stiff climb, but at last she stood breathlessly beside him in the long, flower-dotted grass, and surveyed the view. It was spectacular. They could see for miles in three directions.

'Worth the effort?'

Forgetting their state of armed truce, she sent him a glowing smile. 'Oh, yes. Thanks for bringing me here. I wouldn't have missed it for the world,' she exclaimed, sinking to the grass and clasping her arms around her legs.

'Neither would I,' Kerr agreed in an odd voice, and when Maxi swivelled to look at him questioningly, he was frowning.

'Sometimes, Maxine Ambro, you don't add up.'

'Why?' she questioned with a laugh. 'Because I enjoyed the climb? Because I didn't whinge and carp, and complain of breaking a nail like other rich bitches of your acquaintance?' she mocked.

'Something like that,' he admitted ruefully.

'I'm sorry I couldn't oblige. Perhaps arithmetic isn't your strong point,' she suggested, watching him stretch out beside her.

'Perhaps you put up too good a smokescreen.'

'God, you're impossible!' she exclaimed despairingly, and saw the corners of his lips curl up as he smiled.

'So my mother keeps telling me.'

'You don't have to sound so proud of it. It's a fault, you know, not a virtue.'

Tucking his hands beneath his head, he closed his eyes. 'I never said I was perfect.'

No, Maxi thought wryly, he wasn't perfect, not even close. She watched him in silence. At ease, with his eyes closed, he looked heartbreakingly attractive. She had a ridiculous longing to lie down beside him, have his arms close about her, and let the world drift away. Fingers tightened about her heart, and she felt close to tears. Oh, Maxi, surely you couldn't do anything as foolish as fall in love with this man, she chafed herself.

Even to contemplate it was madness. They ought to lock her up and throw away the key! She lay back and gazed up at the clear blue sky. Loving Kerr would be the greatest folly, and she wasn't a fool. Her instinct for self-preservation was strong, heightened by experience. A wise woman didn't jump from the frying-pan into the fire. She gave herself a good talking-to and followed her own advice. Which Maxi now did, forcing her mind to empty. Hearing nothing but the spiralling call of a lark and the steady breathing of the man beside her, eventually she slept.

When next she opened her eyes, it was because the warmth of the sun had gone from her face. Expecting to see clouds, she focused instead on Kerr's shadowed face as he leaned over her. Her heart thudded as she wondered just how long he had been studying her, and what he was thinking. But, like the sphinx, his expression gave nothing away. The air was so still around them that they could have been the only two people left on earth. Yet the very stillness seemed alive with that special magic which made her feel dangerously alive.

Instantly her defences came up. 'What are you doing?' To her dismay the question faltered and nearly broke.

A lazy smile curved his lips. 'Just enjoying the view.'

Oh, God, when he turned on the heat her blood began to sizzle. Cursing herself for falling asleep and giving him the advantage, she tried to sit up, but he easily foiled the attempt, pushing her back down again. She knew he was stronger than herself, and sought for another means of escape.

'Even though you don't think the inside matches the outside?' she jeered.

His smile deepened as his eyes dropped to her lips. 'What does the inside matter when I like what I see?' He lifted a hand, tracing the neckline of her dress. 'And what I touch.'

Maxi felt her heart start up a new beat, and her mouth went dry. 'Let me go, Kerr,' she ordered huskily, knowing she wasn't just fighting him, but herself too.

His hand moved to frame her face, his thumb tracing caressingly over her lips. 'In a moment.'

A moment would be too late! 'You said you wouldn't force me,' she dredged the words up in a last-ditch attempt for freedom from the spell he was weaving.

Kerr's head came down until his lips just brushed hers. 'I'm not forcing you, darling. All you have to do is push me away,' he mocked softly, and kissed her.

She tried to fight, but it was like going down for the third time. The hands she had gripped his shirt with relaxed, fingers spreading out to trace the strength of his shoulders. With an incoherent murmur, she opened her lips to him and was swept away just as she had despaired she would be. Her arms went round his neck, delighting in his solidity as she returned the ever increasing passion of his kiss. There was no thought, only sensation as his lips left hers and began a journey down the tense arch of her throat to the vee of her breasts.

Maxi could feel her blood coursing thickly through her veins, could feel the heat of Kerr's body scorching hers, and clung on tighter as he unclasped the halter of her dress, brushing it down, exposing her swollen breasts to the worship of his lips. She gasped as she felt him take her flesh into his mouth, biting and teasing until she wanted to scream. She felt molten inside. Nothing had ever made her feel this good. She wanted it to go on and on...

It was only the brush of his hand on her inner thigh which cooled the hot tide of blood in her veins. The sudden return of sanity was like being dropped in ice, and she froze. Dear God, she'd almost...

Kerr's head came up, eyes sceptical and mocking. 'No?'

Trembling with the shock of how close she had come, her throat closed over. 'Damn you!'

His hand left her thigh to mould her breast. 'I very nearly had you that time, didn't I, Maxi? A second ago you were with me all the way!' he taunted, and, sick with mortification, she rolled away, sitting up with her back to him.

Having refastened her dress with trembling fingers, Maxi swung round on him. 'I can't deny it. But the truth is, however much I might have wanted you, I stopped. I'll always stop. I won't have an affair with you, Kerr. How many times do I have to tell you?'

Eyes gleaming, he picked a blade of grass and began to chew it. 'Judging by the last few minutes, a hundred times might not be enough. Do you really expect me to believe you after the way you just responded to me?'

How she would love to wipe that smile from his face! 'Yes, I expect you to believe it, because it just so happens that we don't even like each other.'

'By your own account, you didn't like Ellis either, yet you married him, and presumably went to bed with him.'

It was a direct hit, driving a stake through her heart, leaving her pale with the pain of it. Her response was instinctive, born of a need to hurt back. 'You're right on both counts. I didn't like him but I did sleep with him. He was very inventive. He had a technique which I could never resist. Had he been here with me today, we wouldn't have stopped. I wouldn't have wanted him to!'

'You little bitch!' Kerr's face twisted with anger.

He didn't like that at all. It was a blatant challenge to his manhood. What he didn't know was that it didn't come within a light year of the truth, but she'd rather lose a leg than ever tell him that. Her eyes taunted him. 'What's wrong? Did you think you were the only man who could turn me on?'

Kerr shook his head, once more in the grip of a chilling control. 'I'm not that much of a fool. No, darling, you're the one who's a fool, because you're trying too hard to annoy me. That only makes me wonder why. I think you're afraid you'll enjoy me more than him. Well, it's true, and I'm going to enjoy proving it to you. I'm going to wipe Ellis from your memory as if he had never been, so that when you think of pleasure, the only man you'll ever see is me!'

It was as much a threat as a promise, and Maxi found herself shivering, so cold the sun's rays could have been made of ice. This time she knew she had pushed him too far.

# CHAPTER SEVEN

IT WAS nearly four o'clock when they arrived back at the house again, and the mood in the car had been chilly. Maxi had spent the time deep in thought. It hadn't taken long to realise that she had made a grave error by challenging Kerr that way, but it was too late to back down. She would just have to weather whatever he chose to fling at her. The irony of it was that she would give anything to have the memory of Colin wiped from her mind. Kerr could have been the man to do it, only to give in would concede far too great a victory.

As soon as the car stopped she let herself out, wanting to get away from him to a place where she could lick her wounds and repair her armour. Unfortunately she had forgotten about her hip, the dull ache, which had begun on the return journey, having been pushed to the back of her mind by the other thoughts that swirled there. The long walk had played it up, with the result that she had to clutch at the door to stop herself from falling.

Kerr was at her side in a flash. 'Here, let me help,' he offered, taking her arm, but she shrugged him off.

'I don't need your help. As a matter of fact, I want nothing from you, Kerr, nothing at all,' she refused bluntly.

His nostrils flared on an angry intake of air. 'As it's my fault you're in this condition, I think you're being extremely silly. It's just that prickly pride of yours getting in the way of common sense.'

Maxi drew in a very wobbly breath. 'It may be prickly, but it's mine. So won't you just for once take no for an answer?' she demanded, even as her hand unconsciously rubbed the weakened joint.

Grey eyes followed the movement, lips drawn tight. 'Would it hurt you to accept help now and again?'

Eyes darkened by pain met his. 'From you? It would take me too long to count the strings!' she riposted with heavy irony, and turned away. Which proved to be another error, for the moment she presented her back Kerr stepped forward and swept her up into his arms.

'Then you'd better start counting now,' he advised grimly, and strode into the house with her.

Maxi opened her mouth to protest, then closed it again, words unspoken. To be honest, she did need help, and it was only false pride which made her refuse what was given. So she subsided and let herself relax into the comfort of his arms. And it was a comfort, the breadth of his chest and the strength of his arms making her feel small and cherished. Which was exactly why she had fought him, because she had known she would feel this. It produced an ache that no pain-killer could erase.

She reached that conclusion at the same time as they reached the foot of the stairs, and, with a return of common sense, Maxi cleared her throat. 'You can put me down now.'

Kerr took one look at her determined face and allowed her feet to slide to the floor. With his arm still about her waist, he continued to eye her sardonically. 'There are only two ways you're going up those stairs: either I carry you, or I help you. If you continue to be stubborn, I'll simply throw you over my shoulder and have done with it. So what's it to be?'

She never got the chance to tell him, for as she opened her mouth to scorn his piratical intentions Lady Ambro came hurrying into the hall from the back of the house.

'Oh, Maxine, thank goodness you're back!' she exclaimed, in a flustered tone which was so far from normal that her daughter's heart lurched.

'What is it? What's happened? Is it Father?' she asked quickly, quite inordinately glad to have Kerr behind her. Suddenly their personal troubles had no bearing. Without thinking, she blindly held out her hand, and, when he unhesitatingly took it, felt a surge of emotion there was no time to explore.

'Goodness, no, nothing like that, although it's not good news,' her mother quickly allayed her fears in one direction. 'The police telephoned from London. They got this number from your agent, I think. Oh, darling, your flat has been broken into. They need you to go home and see what's missing.'

Maxi felt the floor tilt and had to sit down abruptly on the bottom stair as her legs gave out. 'But it can't have been. Nobody can get through the doors unless the security man lets them!' she exclaimed, not wanting to believe it. Stunned, her brain refused to work, and it was some seconds before she grasped that a glass was being pressed into her hand.

'Drink it,' Kerr ordered, and she realised, as she obediently took a sip, that he must have gone into the lounge to get some brandy.

Coughing as it caught her throat, she did slowly begin to feel less shocked. Still, it seemed difficult to get her brain working, and she raised a shaky hand to her forehead. 'I'll have to go, I suppose.'

'I'll drive you,' Kerr said decisively.

'There's no need,' she refused, clambering rather inelegantly to her feet, and in the process putting too much weight on her injured leg, nearly toppling over again.

'You seem determined to crumple at my feet.' Kerr's strong hand righted her easily. 'There's every need and you know it. You're in no fit state to drive all the way to town. For one thing you're still in shock, and for another your leg won't take another beating today. So no more arguments.'

Maxi wasn't about to, for he was right. If she insisted, in the state she was in she'd probably crash the car. 'All right, thank you. Actually I think I'll be glad of the company.' She shivered at the idea of a stranger being in her home, and knew she wouldn't want to walk in there on her own. 'I'll just go and change into something warmer.'

Feeling rather like a sleepwalker, she went awkwardly up to her room and mechanically changed into cream denims and a rugby shirt. She assumed they would be away for the night, but any clothes she needed would be at her flat. It only remained to gather up a jacket and her handbag, and she was as ready as she was going to be.

Within half an hour they were on their way, the Porsche eating up the miles. Neither spoke, but Maxi found the soft music Kerr put on the cassette player soothed her nerves. It was strange how this journey differed from the last. Now she felt comforted, the mere fact of his presence making things seem not as bad as they could be. It was a paradox. How could one man make her feel all these different emotions? Drive her to the extremes of anger and passion, then this? The answer seemed to hover in a mist, and she hesitated about dispersing it, for fear of what she might discover.

As they approached the outskirts of the city, Kerr asked for directions, confessing to a knowledge of the area where her flat was situated. When they finally pulled up in the parking area before the building, Maxi was reluctant to get out. But there was no escaping the moment.

'I telephoned your local police before we left,' Kerr informed her as he joined her on the pavement.

'Someone will meet us here shortly. Have you got your key?'

He took it from her when she produced it from her handbag, and let them into the lobby. The guard on duty was one of the night shift, and his commiserations were followed by his belaboured assurances that he would have done something had he seen or heard anything. It was scant comfort, after the event, but she thanked him and passed on to the lift.

Maxi's flat was on the top floor, one of two. Unlocking the door, Kerr threw it wide, and the sight which met their eyes made her gasp aloud. It was as if a bomb had been dropped on the place. Kerr's face was grim as he helped her inside, for this was no ordinary burglary; the place had been very nearly wrecked.

They trailed silently from room to room in mounting horror. In her bedroom, Maxi stared blindly at the mess, for not only had the duvet been slashed, but her entire wardrobe seemed to be a mass of tatters.

'This was no burglar,' Kerr declared in a tone of voice that threatened trouble for somebody. 'Whoever did this had a violent hatred for you.'

Maxi had to swallow hard on a wave of nausea before she could speak. 'But who? Why?'

'You're more likely to know than me. Have you made any enemies?'

One sprang instantly to mind, but was just as instantly disregarded. She pulled a face. 'In my business, you don't always make friends. Let's go in the other room,' she suggested, sickened by the destruction. At least in the lounge the damage was less vicious.

Furniture was overturned and ornaments smashed, but nothing was ripped apart.

'I could do with some coffee,' Kerr announced flatly, nudging what looked like the remains of a Dresden shepherdess with the toe of his shoe.

'I'll make it,' Maxi responded, glad of something to do.

The kitchen had fared best of all, actually having little damage save for a few broken cups. It was like a haven of peace in the midst of a hurricane. Maxi put the kettle on to boil then hesitated as she reached to open a cupboard.

'I suppose it's all right to touch this?'

Kerr pulled out a stool at the breakfast bar. 'We'll risk it, but it's probably best not to touch anything in the other rooms until after we've spoken with the police.' While she busied herself, he idly turned over the large pile of mail she had left on the counter on Friday. 'Do you always get this much?'

Glancing over her shoulder, Maxi shook her head. 'That's quite small, really. We get quite a lot of fan mail, you know. That's what's left after they've weeded it out at the agency. The good stuff, not the hate mail, or the letters from weirdos.'

'Hate mail?' Kerr latched on to that like a terrier. 'Do you get much?'

Carrying across two mugs, she placed one in front of him before pulling out the opposite stool and sliding on to it. 'Only my share, I suppose. Some people can't bear another's success. We don't take it over seriously or else we'd go mad,' she explained, then her eyes widened as she caught his stony expression. 'You surely don't think one of them . . . ?'

'It's a possibility. It could give the police something to go on,' Kerr pronounced thoughtfully, and indeed the detective who arrived not very long afterwards was extremely interested.

On closer inspection of her flat, Maxi couldn't see that anything was actually missing. Such items of valuable jewellery that she possessed were still in the wall safe which was untouched.

'It would appear to be more in the nature of a personal attack, then, miss,' the detective observed, closing his notebook. 'However, we do have some fingerprints which we'll try to match up. We'll look into the mail business too, but if you discover anything missing, or find something that doesn't belong here, or can think of anyone who might bear a grudge, get in touch.' He handed her a card with his name and number, and left.

His departure was like a catalyst. It had been a rotten day, and as Maxi stood there surveying the ruin of her home, everything became too much. She burst into tears. Without hesitation, strong arms gathered her in to a broad chest, cradling her there while she sobbed her heart out, one hand rhythmically stroking her hair. Then when she hiccuped to a stop, a handkerchief was thrust into her hand, and she sniffed and blew inelegantly. She longed to remain where she was, for there had been so much comfort in his arms, but she realised the foolishness of it, and eased herself free.

'Sorry,' she apologised for her emotional outburst diffidently.

'Having seen this, if anyone is entitled to cry, you are,' Kerr declared wryly. 'I almost felt like weeping myself. It must have been a lovely home.'

She heaved a big sigh and pocketed his handkerchief, meaning to wash it and return it. 'It was.'

'I suppose we should look on the bright side, and be thankful whoever did this didn't start chucking jam jars and sauce bottles at the walls. Come on, we may as well start cleaning up. It's bad enough walking in on this once; you don't want to do it again.'

She heartily agreed with that, and disappeared into the kitchen to collect dustpan and broom, and several black plastic bags. Working methodically, righting furniture as they went, it proved remarkably easy to remove the signs of the vandalism. Only the gaps on the shelves where the broken ornaments should have been told the tale. Finally, Maxi left Kerr competently hoovering the carpet while she went back into her bedroom.

Stripping the bed, she dumped everything in the plastic bags. Even had they been repairable, she wouldn't have used them again. There had been so much hate and anger in every cut that she doubted she'd ever want to sleep in the room again. Turning to the wardrobe with a shudder, she was studying the contents when Kerr walked in. He caught sight of her puzzled frown and crossed to her side.

'What is it?'

Maxi fingered a dark green suit. 'I've just noticed that these are undamaged. They're what you'd call my everyday clothes. The ones that were slashed were all my glamour dresses. The ones I use when I'm working.'

'That would certainly back up the theory that someone is jealous of your success.'

Maxi shuddered again, wondering if she would ever stop. 'It's horrible to think of anyone hating me so much. That they've actually been here in my home, going through my personal things. It makes me feel...violated. If they got in once, what's to stop them coming back?'

'That's precisely why you're coming back to my house tonight.'

She caught her breath. Go to his house? Suddenly the tension, which had been missing ever since she had heard the news, returned with a vengeance. However kind he might have been, he was still her adversary.

'That won't be necessary. I can go to a hotel,' she countered quickly, and saw his eyes narrow speculatively. She was pretty sure he knew exactly what she was thinking.

However, much to her surprise, he didn't argue. 'Why don't you get a few things together while I clean up in the kitchen, hmm?' he suggested, with an encouraging smile.

Relieved that for once she had had her own way, she went to do as he said. Walking into the bedroom made her flesh crawl, and she wondered if she'd ever feel safe there again. The thought made her disinclined to linger, and by the time she had collected together all she'd need for an overnight stay, Kerr had tidied up and was waiting in the lounge. Switching off the lights, they left.

When they were in the car and on their way again, Maxi let her gaze drift to Kerr. He handled the car with skill and assurance, with the same consummate ease he handled everything in his life. It wasn't assumed. It was as natural as breathing, and it had supported her when she needed it most. 'I want to thank you for coming with me. It was kind of you.'

'Kindness had nothing to do with it. I owed it to your family,' he replied forthrightly, and she winced at the way it cut her.

With a wry smile of self-derision twisting her lips, because she knew she should have expected his response, she inclined her head. 'Then my family thank you,' she drawled ironically, turning her attention to the world outside. 'I'd forgotten it was high season. Do you think the hotels will have rooms available?'

'I should think so. Tourism isn't what it was a year ago,' Kerr answered as he changed lanes.

Maxi relaxed into her seat. 'I didn't know you had a house here in London.'

To her surprise, considering he was a conscientious driver, Kerr took his eyes from the road to give her a penetrating look. 'Didn't you?' he challenged sardonically. 'I think you must have, or why else didn't you want to go there?'

Maxi frowned. 'Of course I didn't know. How could I? And the only reason I didn't want to go there was because I didn't want to put you out,' she returned swiftly, ending on a lie because the truth was out of the question.

Kerr's attention returned to the traffic. 'Life is full of surprises,' he murmured cryptically, then shrugged. 'I bought the place because I couldn't face all the commuting, although your father didn't seem to mind it. I use my London house during the week, and spend the weekends at the family home. But with my parents now living in New Zealand, and Andy having a place of his own, I rather rattle around in it,' he explained as he neatly threaded the car through the traffic.

'You could sell it,' Maxi suggested.

His shake of the head was firm. 'Uh-uh. I love the old place too much. No, I go more for the idea of getting myself a wife and family.'

Maxi found she was staring out of the window without seeing anything. 'That sounds rather clinical,' she said huskily, aware of her heart giving a sickening lurch.

Kerr steered the car into a quiet street of elegant town houses, drawing up before one in the middle of the row. 'Does it? I prefer to think of it as a matter of common sense. The house needs children, and I want them to be mine. For that I'll need a wife.'

How crazy it was to feel as if her heart was being torn from her at his cynical attitude. 'But what about love?' she argued in a strained voice.

Kerr laughed. 'Love? Love, my dear Maxi, is for fools. It's a romantic nonsense which blinds people to the truth, dressing up lust into something more socially acceptable. Love doesn't exist,' he declared harshly, switching off the engine and the lights, but making no move to get out.

In the gloom, they seemed isolated from the world outside. 'How can you be so certain?' Maxi found her heart was beating achingly fast as she asked the question.

There was just enough light to see grey eyes glittering. 'How? Because I once imagined I was in love,' he answered derisively, and Maxi caught her breath.

'What happened?'

'I came to my senses. I realised I'd made the mistake of confusing love with lust. The object of my—affection—found someone else she wanted more than me. With the blinkers gone, I realised I was well rid of her, and of the notion of love.'

Maxi was so appalled, it was difficult to find words. Surely he could see how wrong he was? 'I'm sorry if she hurt you, Kerr. She obviously didn't love you, but you're far too intelligent to let one bad experience affect your life,' she whispered huskily.

At her words, he climbed abruptly from the car. 'Why should you be sorry?' Kerr exclaimed over his shoulder. 'I'm not. I learnt a lesson I won't forget in a hurry. As you say, I'm far too intelligent to make the same mistake again.'

That wasn't what she had said at all, but she realised the futility of arguing with him. Wearily she followed him out, and only when she stood beside him on the pavement did she look at her surroundings.

'Where are we?' Her eyes quartered the darkened building before her. 'This isn't a hotel,' she accused, turning on him in annoyance.

Taking a firm grip on her arm, he urged her to mount the steps to the front door. 'Full marks for observation. This, as you've probably also guessed by now, is my house.'

She had indeed fathomed that out, and consequently resisted him at every step. 'You said you'd take me to a hotel!'

'Uh-uh! You said that, I didn't,' he corrected. 'I said you were coming home with me.'

A reminder she didn't need, but which had her grinding her teeth in impotent anger. She couldn't run away because she didn't even know where they were. Yet when she reluctantly stood beside him as he hunted for the latchkey she experienced an uncanny sensation of *déjà vu*. Her heart unaccountably picked up its pace. The feeling increased as she followed Kerr inside. Her breath caught in her throat. Everything was unfamiliar, and yet so much in the right place that it was instantly familiar. She hesitated in the doorway, and found Kerr watching her, a strangely intent look in his eye.

'Something wrong?' he queried, voice softly mocking.

It was almost as if he was waiting for something, and she walked further in. 'I don't...' She broke off, eyes going to a door at the end of the hall. Suddenly she knew. One look beyond that barrier would confirm her staggering idea. Without waiting for permission, she walked swiftly to the door and went through into the room. It was a library, but the books didn't hold her attention; that was fixed on the glass doors in the far wall. They opened at her touch, and Maxi found herself in the leafy shadows of a Victorian conservatory.

Without her volition, her feet carried her forwards, to where she knew, out of sight, stood a wrought-iron seat. There she stopped, eyes mirroring an unforgotten pain. 'It was your house.' The words issued tonelessly to the silent figure she sensed behind her.

For a moment he didn't answer. 'I thought you knew.'

Maxi's fingers tightened around the cold metal. 'How could I? I didn't know who the house belonged to, and we never did exchange names, did we? You were just——'

'A masked figure who happened to pique your interest for a few hours,' he interrupted roughly, and her throat closed over.

It had been more than that, so much more, but what point was there in telling him, when so much else had happened? Their lives had touched for a while and then parted. She hadn't seen him again until two days ago, hadn't allowed herself to think of him in all that time, because it would only have heightened her sense of loss. Then she had blanked him out because of Colin, and now she did so because he was no longer the Harlequin of her dreams.

It became imperative not to reveal the true depths of her turmoil. Fixing a faint smile on her lips, she turned to face him. 'Which is what I was to you, too. A fleeting moment out of time.'

'Which neither of us has forgotten. You stirred me then as you stir me now,' Kerr admitted huskily.

'But it's too late. Seven years ago, who knows what would have happened? We're not the same people.'

'Tell me something, Maxi, just as a matter of interest. Would you have settled for me if Ellis hadn't turned up?' Kerr asked conversationally, moving round to face her.

Maxi felt her heart contract. 'Kerr, there's nothing to be gained by this,' she protested helplessly.

He ignored her, catching her under the chin with fingers that hurt. 'You never intended seeing me again after that night, did you, darling?' he mused silkily.

'Please, stop it,' she pleaded, moisture making her eyes glitter.

'Why? I would have thought you'd enjoy knowing just how much of a fool I was. After all, that was the purpose of your little come-on out here where it's delightfully secluded. Wasn't I supposed to be so smitten that I couldn't get you out of my mind?' he taunted cuttingly.

'No,' she denied hoarsely, her hand rising to lock around his wrist, yet unable to move him.

'Why don't I believe you? Perhaps because you know so well how to tantalise a man. Like giving him your telephone number, but never being there to answer. Oh, yes, I rang,' he confirmed as he felt her jerk of surprise. 'Why not? You'd given me the sort of come-on even a blind man couldn't mistake. What sort of man could resist the lure of a mystery woman? I was determined to find you, although I must admit, I didn't expect to discover you right on my very own doorstep!'

If she'd known he was there ... But what was the use in tormenting herself? She couldn't have done anything differently. 'This is all so worthless,' she insisted, choked.

His lips twisted unpleasantly. 'My thoughts exactly when I saw you set to work on Ellis, just as you had with me.'

Oh, God! It hadn't been the same at all. She felt nothing for Colin. Nothing. To hear him compare what they had shared with the sham of her later actions brought a wrenching agony of heart and mind. Dammit, she had loved him! Why couldn't he tell the difference? Why couldn't he see that she still——? The self-torment ended abruptly as his voice broke into her thoughts.

'So tell me, Maxi, how many others have fallen foul of your net?' he enquired dulcetly.

Maxi finally found the strength to push his hand away, meeting the derision in his eyes with boldly raised chin. 'Why are you doing this? What difference does it make now?' she demanded tautly, balling her hands into fists to quell their shaking.

Kerr slipped his hands into his pockets. 'None, of course. Except, as one of the fortunate ones who's thanking his lucky stars for a narrow escape, I did wonder if I'm in a minority of one or not.'

Was there no end to the ways he could find to inflict wounds? 'Well, you can keep on wondering!'

Kerr laughed shortly. 'Frankly, darling, I can't be bothered to waste the time or energy,' he dismissed, and glanced at his watch. 'It's late. You'd better come back through. I'll get us something to eat,' he suggested evenly, as if they'd just been talking about the weather.

Maxi felt the urge to burst into hysterical laughter. Having just put her through those minutes of withering scorn, how could he possibly expect her to sit down and eat with him?

'If it's all the same to you, I'd rather just go to my room.' With the thought of food nauseating her, she wouldn't be able to eat anyway.

Kerr raked her pale face with a probing glance, and didn't press the point. Back once more in the hall, he picked up her case and silently led the way upstairs, showing her to a room overlooking the garden.

'You should be comfortable here. It has its own bathroom. If you should feel hungry later, feel free to use the kitchen.'

The indifference of his cool politeness struck a chill through her. Not to be outdone, she somehow found an icy smile. 'I'm sure I'll be fine. Thank you for your kindness.'

He didn't miss the irony, and stared at her for a long moment before inclining his head in acknowledgement. He left with a brief goodnight. As he went, so did her strength, and she sank down on to the side of the bed wearily. It had been a day of shocks, and this last one the most devastating. To come here and find it was the scene of that most unforgettable meeting still sent shockwaves through her. It had been the happiest night of her life, for she had fallen in love with a mysterious stranger. It had been magical, almost unreal, but, for all that, very, very real. She hadn't been able to think of anyone else. She'd longed for him to get in touch. Then...

Maxi firmed her lips into a tight line. Then Colin had happened. There was no point in crying about it. She had made a decision and kept to it. Nothing had changed. Not even knowing how Kerr had hated her for seven years could change one little thing. She mustn't let him get to her.

With grim determination to follow her own advice, she gathered up her night things, taking them into the bathroom. But once under the shower, first one raking sob and then another escaped from her, and it was impossible to hold back any longer the tears she had always refused to shed. They mingled with the spray that trickled its way down her cheeks. Only when there were no more tears left to shed did she step out of the cubicle and dry herself, slipping into a silk nightdress. As worn out as she felt, she knew she would be unable to sleep, so she didn't bother to try, just curled up on top of the bed.

Silence descended on the house. She wondered what Kerr was doing. Would he be thinking of her, just as she was thinking of him? No, why should he? She was just the woman who betrayed him with another man. The phrase almost made her heart stop. *Betrayed him with another man* ... What was it Kerr had said when she'd asked him about love? He didn't believe in it because the woman he thought he'd loved had found someone else she wanted more.

Sitting up abruptly, Maxi pressed her fingers to her temples, willing her thoughts not to fly off in all directions, but to be logical. At the time she'd thought he was talking of someone else, but what if...? Would it have been so impossible for him to have fallen in love with *her*? After all, she had fallen in love with him that night. It would explain the depth of his anger. Dear lord, if it was true, then no wonder he hated her. He had known everything, seen everything. She could imagine his shock, his disgust. How could he have known it was only an act? They hadn't had time to get to know each other. No wonder he thought she had been playing him for a fool.

But she hadn't been, and suddenly it was vitally important that he should know that. Oh, she didn't think for a minute that it would make him stop hating her, but what he had seen had made him stop believing in love. That was the injustice of it. She was the only one who could put the record straight, and in so doing stop him from missing out on that most precious of human emotions.

Without giving herself time for second thoughts, she swung her legs over the side of the bed and reached for her robe. Barefoot, she let herself out of the room and made for the stairs. She knew Kerr hadn't come up to bed, for she would have heard him, so he had to be downstairs somewhere. At the foot of the stairs she glanced about her. There was light coming from a room on the right side of the hall, and she padded over to it. Yet when she stepped into what turned out to be a study, she couldn't see him.

'What can I do for you, Maxi?'

Just as she was about to leave, Kerr's disembodied voice made her jump and turn back. In time to see the large chair at the other side of the desk, which she had thought was empty, swing round to reveal his seated figure. He must have been staring out into the darkened garden, and seen her reflection in the window.

Her nerves fluttered, but she had never been one to run away from a task, however difficult it might be. Had she been, she doubted if she'd be in the position she now found herself in. She slowly approached the desk, aware of his eyes following every graceful step. Halting before him, she linked her fingers so that they almost looked like praying hands. 'I want to talk to you.'

'I can see you've gone to the trouble of dressing down for the occasion,' Kerr drawled ironically, setting her teeth on edge instantly.

'I'm serious, Kerr,' she snapped back edgily, wishing she'd dressed again before coming down.

She didn't have to see them to know his brows lifted. 'Oh, I can see that you are,' he agreed drily. 'Would we be more comfortable on the couch?'

Catching her breath on a blistering reply, she forced herself not to march out of the room. 'No, we damn well would not!' she said tautly. 'This is important. The least you could do is stop making asinine remarks.'

Not by a millimetre did his expression change. All that moved was the hand that had been resting on the arm of the chair, which lifted to support his chin. 'OK, I'm listening.'

Having gained his attention, she took a steadying breath. 'I think it's about time we were honest with each other,' she began carefully.

'Are you sure you know how?' he interjected scornfully, then raised his other hand placatingly. 'Go on.'

Maxi realised she should have guessed he wouldn't make this easy for her, but it only strengthened her resolve not to give way. 'There's something I need to know, and there's no other way I know of getting an answer than just coming right out and asking. So-o, I want you to tell me if I was the woman you said you fell in love with.'

For a while it seemed he wasn't going to answer one way or the other, but then he laughed. 'Well, well, well. You are being honest with yourself if you recognised yourself from that description!'

She flushed, as he had no doubt intended she should. She held on to her temper, but leant both hands on the edge of the desk, to bring herself into eye contact. 'Is that a yes or a no?' she charged grittily.

Kerr sat forward too. Resting one elbow on the leather surface, he reached across to trail one long finger around the lacy neck of her nightdress. 'Why do you want to know?' he countered throatily. 'Idle curiosity, or is it another game?'

Gasping, she pulled back, but not before her nipples had responded to that blatant caress, jutting proudly against the insubstantial fabric in a manner he must surely have seen. Seething with equal parts of anger and embarrassment, she hastily clutched the folds of her robe around her. 'Neither! I mistakenly thought we could have a reasonable conversation. I was wrong.' Not for the first time, but probably for the last. She turned, and had actually taken a step before his voice stopped her.

'Hell, there's no reason why I shouldn't admit it. After all, everybody is allowed at least one mistake. The trick is to learn from it. Yes, I was once foolish enough to think I loved you, Maxi.'

The statement brought her swinging back to face him. 'That's what I wanted to tell you. Loving someone *isn't* foolish, Kerr,' she argued strongly.

He didn't answer immediately. After a moment he rose, going to stand at the window with his back to her. 'You're speaking as an expert, are you? As someone who knows what love is?' he taxed her, in a voice that was, for once, devoid of sarcasm.

It encouraged her to continue. 'Yes, I do know what I'm talking about, because I fell in love with you, too, Kerr.' Her confession fell into a pool of silence.

'You... fell in love with me,' he repeated tonelessly, turning slowly. She knew he was watching her, but she couldn't see his face because the draped curtain threw him into shadow. 'You know, seven years ago that was what I wanted to hear, but it's pretty hard to believe after all this time.'

Maxi shrugged her shoulders helplessly. 'I know.'

'So why are you telling me now?'

It was the critical question, and she answered care-fully. 'Because I hate to think you're turning your back on love because of me.'

At the window, Kerr stood as still as a statue. 'And that's your only reason?' he probed softly.

She frowned faintly, trying to cut through the gloom in order to see him better. 'What other reason could there be?'

'Perhaps you're hoping I might still love you after all,' he offered, still in that same controlled voice.

Maxi shook her head. 'I know you don't.'

Another silence fell, dragging on until she felt her nerves tense. 'You're saying you want me to be free to love again, is that it?' Kerr eventually responded. 'But I no longer believe in love.'

Instantly she stepped closer. 'But you could, if you just let yourself. There's no reason not to,' she insisted.

'Because you weren't playing me for a fool?'

Now, at last, he was beginning to understand. 'Yes. I loved you, Kerr. Of course I didn't make a fool of you. I really did love you,' she repeated earnestly, and finally he moved.

Laughter echoed round the room. 'And you say it with just the right catch in your voice too!' Kerr derided, stepping into the light so that she could see the contempt on his face.

Maxi rocked back on her heels, realising far, far too late, that she had been tricked. Humiliation brought hot colour to her cheeks. 'You bastard!'

With a harsh laugh he rounded his desk, resting his weight back on it and crossing his arms. 'Temper, temper,' he cautioned mockingly. 'What were you really hoping for, darling? That I'd fall for your bag of tricks all over again?'

Shaking as she was, she used every muscle to make certain he should never know it. 'I told you the truth.'

Kerr shook his head sadly. 'I know, I'm a strange man. I really should believe you, but somehow I can't help remembering how you were winding yourself around Ellis just a couple of days later. Or are you going to tell me that was a figment of my imagination?'

She didn't speak, she couldn't, nor could she move when he pushed himself upright and closed the gap between them. He raised a hand to run his fingers caressingly over her face, eyes following the movement as if committing the sight of her to memory.

'That may be your idea of love, Maxi, but it isn't mine. Call it lust, and I'd be more inclined to believe you. We turned each other on, we still do. If the whole point of tonight's little exercise was to offer yourself to me, there was no need to call it love. I wouldn't have refused you.' His hand slowly trailed down to her breast, feeling the betraying hardness of its peak as, against her will, her body responded. His lips curved. 'I still won't. So, is that what you're doing, Maxi, offering yourself?'

Meeting his glittering eyes with her own flashing their own brand of scorn, she picked up his hand by the wrist and dropped it away as if it was something particularly nasty. Her smile was wintry. 'I'm not yet so desperate for a man that I'd turn to you,' she declared, determined to salvage what was left of her pride.

If she had expected to wound him, she was disappointed. He stepped back with a lazy smile. 'Then you might as well go back to bed, Maxi,' he advised, turning away from her and picking up a paper from his desk. 'But in case you should change your mind, my room is at the end of the corridor. Pleasant dreams,' he added over his shoulder.

How she wished she could find something withering to say, but she was all out of pithy replies. Maintaining her dignity, she said nothing, merely turned her back and left. The stairs seemed endless, and they swam mistily as she climbed them. Once more in her room, she threw herself down on the bed, eyes staring blindly at the ceiling. She should have known he wouldn't believe her, but it hurt that he couldn't see she had been telling the truth. Well, that was the last time she stuck her neck out to help him. The sooner they parted company, the better.

She rolled on to her stomach, and her fist thudded into the pillow. Damn him. Damn him to hell.

# CHAPTER EIGHT

MAXI climbed down stiffly from the train and reached inside for her case. She had hardly slept after their late-night talk, and there had been no rest on the train either. Which, she thought with grim amusement, was probably poetic justice for making the arbitrary decision to take the train in the first place. She hadn't consulted Kerr, merely left him a note to say what she was doing, convincing herself her bad manners were justified because he wouldn't thank her for having to miss a working day in order to drive her home.

As it turned out, she was far too early for the train, and had had to change twice, with the inevitable hanging about, so that she was weary and irritable by the time she reached her stop. Hindsight told her it would have been simpler to take the lift Kerr had been bound to offer, but she hadn't felt able to. Not when she had realised, during that long sleepless night, that she was still very much in love with him.

Hopelessly in love. Hopelessly, stupidly, madly in love. Why else could he have hurt her so, driven her to the highest peaks and the lowest lows? Why else should she care that her actions had made him give up on love? It shouldn't have mattered. Nothing should have mattered if she didn't care for him. Then, of course, it had been impossible to ignore the truth which had been fighting to emerge into her consciousness. She loved him, and there wasn't a thing she could do about it. If all that he had said and done couldn't kill it, then nothing ever would. How she would come to terms with the futility of it was her problem. She hadn't yet found the answer.

Nor did there appear to be an answer to the fact that the taxi rank was empty.

'Damn, damn, damn!'

'I'll take that,' an all-too-familiar voice spoke from behind her, and a strong hand came to rest over hers on the handle of her case.

Maxi very nearly jumped out of her skin as she found herself staring up into an inimical face. 'Kerr?' Her voice shook with shock, a fact he registered with grim satisfaction.

'The car's over here,' he went on, taking the case easily from her slackened grasp, and striding off so that she had to very nearly trot to keep up with him.

'What are you doing here?'

'Going out of my way to give you a lift,' he supplied caustically, opening the boot, and would have tossed her case inside had she not made a grab for it.

She had got over the first shock of seeing him, and although her heart had leapt crazily at the sight of him it only served to warn her she was wise to keep her distance. 'I don't want a lift, as you would have found out if you read my note.'

'I read it,' he said shortly, and, with ridiculous ease, retook the case, shutting it in the boot before pointedly opening the passenger side door. 'Get in.'

She stood her ground. She might be foolish enough to still love him, but she didn't have to obey his every command! 'I'm taking a taxi.'

He looked far from impressed. 'You have two choices, Maxi. Either we discuss this in private or we have a stand-up fight in the street for everyone to see. Frankly, after the morning I've had, I'm in the mood for either.'

Glancing around, she discovered they had already attracted a deal of attention. If she didn't want to cause a great deal more, then she had better take the course of least resistance. Without another word, but sending him a look which spoke volumes, she took her seat.

Silently he climbed in beside her, and just as silently started the car and put it in motion, although his movements revealed that he was furiously angry.

Maxi, aware now of just how vulnerable she was, didn't mind at all. There was safety in anger, less chance of her betraying herself. Besides, a small honest voice whispered in her ear, she rather liked fighting with him. There were times when it was quite exhilarating. At least she had his undivided attention, and sometimes she even won.

She allowed another mile to speed by before saying coolly, 'I can't imagine why you're angry, but you'd better say something before you explode.'

His answer was to glance quickly into the rear-view mirror before steering the car off the road on to the verge. 'I'm angry because you're bloody infuriating. Instead of taking the usual route home, I've had to trek across half Dorset to fetch you,' he thundered.

Far from quailing, Maxi raised her eyebrows. 'Nobody asked you to. You could have stayed and gone to work instead of charging off after me.'

Releasing his belt, Kerr turned threateningly in his seat. 'Had you bothered to ask me, I would have told you I wasn't going to work—that I have a few days' leave owing, which I'm taking this week to put my house into some kind of order.'

Which left her with nothing to say, save a very inadequate, 'Oh.'

'Oh, indeed,' he drawled, visibly relaxing. Making himself comfortable against his door, he tipped his head curiously. 'So, care to tell me just why you were running away?'

Maxi's lips parted on a sharp intake of breath. 'You are the most conceited man I've ever met! I wasn't running away,' she denied, preferring to describe it to herself as a tactical retreat—neither of which she would admit to aloud. 'I decided to make my own way home because I didn't want to bother you,' she expanded, and Kerr laughed self-mockingly.

'You bother me all the time,' he declared, making her blink in surprise. 'Your very presence anywhere on this planet bothers me.'

And he didn't like it one little bit, that was obvious. 'Sorry, but I'm not about to "shuffle off this mortal coil" any quicker than I have to. Not for you or anyone else,' she riposted tartly.

This time his smile was genuine, but there was a brooding look in his eye as he reached out to turn her towards him with surprisingly gentle fingers under her chin. 'Why is it I get the feeling the world would be a duller place if you did? You anger me quicker than anyone else I know, so that when I'm with you I either want to throttle you or kiss you!'

Her eyes were drawn to his as if by a powerful magnet. She knew she was getting way out of her depth, but a powerful force was urging her on. 'Is that what you want to do now, throttle me?' she asked dangerously.

Tantalisingly, his thumb began to caress her bottom lip. Somewhere at the back of his eyes a flame flickered as he laughed huskily. 'Guess again,' he invited, in that dangerous tone which set her heart fluttering in her chest, and brought his lips crushing down on hers.

It was madness, but she craved his kiss as a thirsting person craved water. Unable to move because of her belt, she wouldn't have tried anyway because behind that heated exchange she recognised an emotion bordering on desperation. She knew he didn't want to feel this, but couldn't help himself. She knew that emotion so well. Therefore, she could no more deny him her lips than stop breathing, and, in giving, received. What began as a fierce assault melted into a slow, erotic exploration of the honeyed sweetness of her mouth as she opened to his insistent tongue. Her hand came up to tangle in his hair, holding him to her when his lips left hers to plunder the tender cord of her neck. It was so beautiful. So hopeless.

'Damn you, Maxi,' he muttered raggedly against her scented flesh. 'How can you keep saying no, when everything in you cries out yes? You go up in flames in my arms!' Kerr pulled her head back, and she found herself looking up into eyes that were like storm-tossed seas.

Her neck ached, but not nearly as much as her heart. 'Because you despise me. Because you hate yourself for wanting me. Because I know that if I give in to you I'll end up feeling as cheap as you think I am, and I'll hate myself.'

His face closed up angrily. 'Even if I say I'll still respect you in the morning?' he taunted, and she drew in a sharp breath.

'While you can still say those kind of things to me, Kerr, the answer will always be no,' she said as evenly as she could.

'You expect me to believe that, when every time I touch you I know damn well I could change your mind?' he insisted.

She paled at that truth. He could do it so easily, but at what cost to them both? 'Only by force. The force you said you wouldn't use,' she reminded him. 'Or are you saying you've changed your mind? That you're quite prepared to rape me? Because it will have to be that, Kerr. I'll never come to you willingly.'

Kerr went quite still. 'No, damn you, it won't be rape. I've never in my life forced a woman, and I don't intend to start with you.'

His hands dropped away, and Maxi sank weakly back into her seat. 'I'm glad to hear it.'

'And I'll be glad to hear exactly what it is you are holding out for. Marriage?'

'What?' Dear God, hadn't anything she'd said got through? 'I ought to take you up on that, just to make you suffer, Kerr Devereaux! As it is, I wouldn't marry you if you were the only man left on earth!' she exclaimed, feeling the tension in her head turn to an ache, an ache that was echoed in her heart. 'Can we please go now?'

With angry movements Kerr fastened his belt and started the engine, but didn't engage a gear. 'This is far from over,' he warned tersely, and, with less than his usual smoothness, set them on their way again.

Maxi didn't bother to answer. Battling his dislike and anger was bad enough, without having to fight her own response to him. She felt bruised and battered, and longed to get home, but they still had a twenty-minute ride ahead of them before they reached the village. It felt more like an hour when eventually the spire of the church came into view.

Relieved that they would be home soon, and praying that Fliss would not be anywhere in sight, thus eliminating any need for pretence, Maxi let her gaze drift to the busy main street. As she did so, a male figure emerged from the newsagent's. For a moment, as the car swept past, she couldn't think why it seemed so familiar. Then it hit her, and with a gasp she turned in her seat to get another look. But already the man had disappeared from view. Heart thumping anxiously, she slumped back into her seat.

Kerr spared her a glance, then another when he caught sight of her pale face. 'What is it? What did you see?'

She bit her lip hard. 'It's crazy, but I could have sworn I just saw Colin,' she answered, before she could think better of it.

'Ellis?' Kerr's voice reverberated with dislike. 'What would he be doing here?'

Maxi curled her hands into fists and told herself to be sensible. 'I don't know,' she said, more to herself than to Kerr. As the first shock began to fade, logic returned. 'It couldn't have been him, not here.' A fact that brought a shiver of relief, because Colin was the very last person she wanted to see, ever again.

'I'd like to think you're right, but we can't be sure,' Kerr pointed out grimly.

Maxi was breathing easier now. 'I can. Colin isn't in this country,' she declared with absolute confidence.

'I thought you said you haven't seen him?' Kerr's voice was heavy with suspicion, and she realised she had revealed more than she intended.

'I told you the truth, but that doesn't mean I don't know where he is. Colin isn't in England. Take my word for it,' she advised hardly.

'I might, if I knew how you can be so certain,' Kerr demurred.

Unseen, Maxi pulled a wry face. She could be certain because the last time she had seen Colin he had been about to begin a long prison sentence—thanks almost entirely to her. But that was another story.

'Let's just say I know him better than you do, and leave it at that,' she evaded neatly, and was saved further cross-questioning when they turned into the drive a few seconds later.

No sooner had the car drawn to a halt before the house than her mother was on the top step waiting for them.

'Darling, you look so tired!' she exclaimed as Maxi mounted the steps, and swept her daughter into a fond embrace. 'Was it terribly bad, dear?'

'Bad enough,' Kerr interjected, bringing up the rear with Maxi's case. 'Whoever it was had had a good go at trashing the place, but nothing was actually missing. The police think it looks more like a personal attack.'

'Good gracious!' Lady Ambro looked justifiably horrified. 'What are they doing about it?'

'Checking into Maxi's hate mail,' he replied, shepherding them inside, setting the case down by the door.

'Hate mail? Oh, Maxine, you never should have got into such a dangerous profession!' her mother declared protectively. 'I can't bear to think of you living all alone in the city.'

To have her own thoughts spoken aloud didn't increase Maxi's confidence. Nevertheless, she smiled. 'It's all right, really. Nothing like this has ever happened before. I'm sure the police will soon get whoever did it. It will probably turn out to be just a crank.'

Her mother looked doubtful. 'If you say so, dear, but I don't mind admitting I won't feel comfortable until they get him. Come into the lounge. Mrs Toomey has just made tea. You must be dying for a cup. Will you join us, Kerr?'

He gave her a smile. 'I'd love to, thanks, Bernice.'

'Then would you mind going to the library and reminding John about the tea? Or it will get cold.'

Maxi followed her mother as Kerr walked off. Collapsing into a corner of the nearest couch, she accepted her cup gratefully.

'It was very good of Kerr to go with you like that, wasn't it? Although it's exactly the kind of thing he would do,' Lady Ambro declared, and Maxi looked up with a wry smile. She knew the signs which told her her mother was intent on matchmaking, but how could she blame her when they had given her cause to think the match was possible?

'Yes, he can be kind,' she agreed with a heavy sigh.

Her mother looked at her intently. 'What's the matter, dear?' she asked gently. 'I thought you liked Kerr?'

Maxi kept her eyes rigidly on the slowly swirling tea. Like was such an insipid word for what she felt. 'I do, but . . .'

Reaching out a hand, Lady Ambro gave her daughter's free hand a squeeze. 'But you think Colin will always come between you? Well, darling, that might well be so if you don't tell him the truth. You'll be doing him an injustice if you think he won't understand.'

If only it was that simple. Kerr might well understand, but it still wouldn't make him feel anything more for her than a reluctant passion. She had been through too much to settle for half-measures. If she had to make a commitment, then it would be all or nothing. She couldn't give less, and wouldn't accept less. However, it was far too complicated a problem to discuss over tea, so she merely said,

'I'm just waiting for the right time.'

'Well, don't wait too long, dear. Kerr is a very eligible man. Someone else might come along and snap him up right under your nose!' her mother chided, then was distracted by the sound of approaching feet. 'Ah, here they are at last,' she declared.

Only it wasn't just the two men who appeared in the doorway. Fliss and Andy were with them—a much more relaxed Fliss than the woman Maxi had encountered over the weekend. Although still a little reserved, she sympathised over the burglary. That began a general discussion, and Maxi was both amused and warmed by the proposals put forward for her safety.

Eventually a lull fell, and into it Kerr said, 'Maxi and I thought we'd take you two out for dinner tonight.'

Maxi wasn't the only one who looked up in surprise. It was going a bit further than Fliss was ready for, but even as she opened her mouth to protest their mother was ahead of her.

'What a lovely idea. You young people should go out on your own.'

Her youngest daughter's smile waved considerably. 'Of course, but I should think Maxi feels far too tired after the last twenty-four hours.'

Maxi would have been quite happy to accept the let-out, but Kerr had other ideas. 'Nonsense. She needs cheering up. A good meal in pleasant company will be just what the doctor ordered, eh, Andy?'

'Oh, absolutely,' his brother agreed, laughing, and there was nothing either woman could do except accept gracefully.

Later, when everyone had dispersed, Maxi met Kerr in the hall. He was just in the act of putting the phone down. 'Breaking a date?' she taunted, and he sent her a wolfish smile.

'Now is that likely, when I have eyes only for you?' he retorted ironically, and she rolled her own eyes.

'Where you're concerned, anything is likely. That was a very clever move you made earlier.' He had very neatly linked them as a pair.

'I thought so. It was too good an opportunity to miss, and the strategy seems to be working,' Kerr agreed, crossing to where she stood by the stairs.

'Good. That means this farce will soon be over.'

Sliding his hands into the pockets of his jeans, he shook his head, eyes gleaming. 'You know you don't really mean that, darling,' he argued in a tone designed to set her nerves tingling.

His closeness was a threat her survival instinct said she should back off from, but she resisted. 'I do mean it.'

Again he shook his head. 'No, you don't, because you'll no longer have Fliss for an excuse to go out with me. You'll have to stop kidding yourself then.'

Maxi uttered a disbelieving laugh. 'I'm not kidding anyone, least of all myself. When this is over, I'll be only too relieved to have to see very little of you. Christmas and Easter will be quite sufficient.'

Kerr sobered, expression assured. 'It will never be enough.'

Loving him as she did, she already knew that, but to admit it was a folly she wouldn't commit. 'Are you sure you aren't referring to yourself?' she countered tersely.

'You keep talking about me, what I want, or what I need. I think you should put your own house in order before you start on mine! Now excuse me, I intend to go and have a rest before embarking on this marvellous evening you've planned for us all!'

His voice followed her upstairs. 'You can keep running, Maxi, but every time you look over your shoulder I'll be there, waiting.'

The dinner at Lyme Regis had been a surprise success, Maxi decided hours later, as she strolled slowly along the Cobb. The breeze off the sea made her shiver again. Tonight she had chosen to wear black trousers with a white sleeveless silk blouse, neither of which were designed for a chilly night. Glancing up at the still starlit sky, she wondered if the weather might be on the change. Then she glanced over her shoulder to see if Kerr was coming. The four of them had been going for a walk when he had been called back to take a telephone call at the restaurant. The manager had sent one of the waiters after them because the caller had said it was urgent. He had told them to go on and he'd join them, but that had been almost ten minutes ago.

Kerr was nowhere in sight, but she waved to Fliss and Andy who had declined the longer walk in favour of a sheltered seat, and carried on. She was almost at the end now, and it seemed a shame not to go on. She'd take a quick look, and if Kerr still wasn't back they'd have to go and find him.

A little ahead of her, a lone male figure came up the steps from the lower level and stood directly in her path, staring out to sea. As she hesitated, wondering whether it might not be better to turn back, the man suddenly turned to face her. Her gasp of shock died under the wash of the waves, and she stood as if turned to stone. Even in the darkness, it was possible to see her ex-husband smile.

'Nice night for a stroll,' Colin Ellis observed in a voice she had hoped she'd forgotten, as if the last seven years had never happened.

Though she knew the wisest course of action was to turn and walk away, her feet appeared rooted, and wouldn't obey. His reappearance had shocked her, just as he had doubtless intended. All she could think of was that he shouldn't be here. He should be in prison, not here, facing her on this lonely strip of stone.

Her voice sounded rough and unused as she forced herself to speak. 'How did you get here?' she asked, realising that it *had* been him she had seen in the village earlier.

Colin slipped his hands into his pockets, the smile fading to reveal a nasty edge. 'I followed you, of course. You seemed to enjoy your meal. You were so busy, you never even noticed me tucked away in a corner.'

The knowledge that he had been there all the time, watching them, made her stomach heave. 'That isn't what I meant,' she countered in a constricted tone. 'How did you get to England? How did you...?' The last question tailed off, because she was suddenly very afraid.

Colin had no trouble finishing for her. 'Get out of prison? Easy, lovey, it's called parole. Time off for good behaviour. You didn't think about that, did you, when you conspired to put me away?' he jeered.

She winced inwardly. No, she hadn't thought of it. She'd been too glad to see him put inside, too relieved that her marriage was over. She hadn't given a thought to parole, or what he might do if he gained it. She thought about it now, though, and it chilled her blood. She had to have time to think.

'Listen, I'm not on my own. Kerr's just down there.' She nodded shorewards.

Colin laughed. 'Oh, no, he isn't, babe. He's answering a call from a friend of mine. That should keep him busy for—oh, at least another five minutes.'

She shivered. Like the clever con artist he was, he had found a way to get her on her own. Which meant he had to have a reason to do so. 'What do you want?' she demanded thickly, recalling all the reasons why she had so disliked him. He wasn't quite as handsome now, the years in prison taking their inevitable toll.

'You're too intelligent not to know. I want my revenge, sweetie. No one, but no one takes away six years from me without paying for it!' he told her viciously. 'I've been watching you, planning what I'd do to make you suffer the way I did. Which reminds me—your sister has grown into a beauty.'

The inherent threat returned movement to her feet, and she stepped forward in angry defence. 'Stay away from her, do you hear me? Stay away from all my family!'

He laughed. 'You always did come out of your corner fighting.'

Oh, yes, she'd fought him, only he had always hit harder. 'I despise you!'

That only seemed to amuse him further. 'You always did, that was half the pleasure. I bet this Kerr doesn't have half the trouble getting you into bed that I did. In love with him, are you? That's really funny, because he was interested in you, too, back in the old days. Couldn't take his eyes off you. Of course, you were far too involved with pretending to be hot for me to see him pining for you!' He laughed again, but it held a ring that brought the hairs up on her flesh.

To know he had seen more than she had brought her temper to the boil. Without volition her hand shot out, and would have dealt him a stinging slap if he hadn't seen it coming and caught her wrist, twisting it punishingly until she gasped aloud.

'Naughty, naughty! You don't want to make me angry, love, you know that. You'd better remember that next time it might not be your brakes that fail,' he warned chillingly, and she paled.

Not until that very moment had she even suspected anything so macabre. '*You* tampered with the brakes of my car?'

Colin shrugged. 'I wanted to teach you a much needed lesson. I thought of nothing else all the time I was locked up.' The memory was clearly far from pleasant, for his face turned to stone.

Maxi pulled her arm free with a jerk. 'Don't expect me to apologise!'

Colin swiftly closed the gap between them. 'I don't. I expect you to pay. So if you don't want anything to happen to lover-boy, you'll do exactly as I say!' he ordered sharply.

Her chin jutted. 'I'm not afraid of you! Now I know what you've done, I'll go to the police!'

'Do it, and your bloke will have an accident too,' he warned, eyes glittering feverishly, so that she knew he was on something. 'If you want your family safe, all you have to do is come back to me, Maxi.'

Her instinct was to give a scornful refusal, but she knew better than to be so rash. She needed to use caution in order to gain precious thinking time. 'You've got to give me time. I can't make a decision just like that.'

He didn't like what she said, but as he was about to argue, his attention was caught by something he saw over her shoulder, and he stepped back, swearing. 'OK, you've got until tomorrow. I'll ring you at home at noon. This time I don't want to get your mother when I ring,' he advised, revealing that he had been the mysterious caller on Saturday. 'Say yes at noon, Maxi, or all bets are off, and you can blame yourself for whatever happens to him.' He nodded behind her, then crossed swiftly to the edge and the steps down to the lower level. In seconds he might never have been there.

Only Maxi knew he had, for every word he had spoken echoed in her brain. Uppermost was his threat to hurt Kerr. It was a knife in her heart. He'd do it, she knew that. He seemed unbalanced in a way he never had before. What he suggested was anathema to her, but the thought of anything happening to Kerr sent more daggers to wound her. There was no way she could ever go back to Colin, but what on earth could she do to prevent his reprisal? She had to think!

Approaching footsteps abruptly brought her out of her dark thoughts. She turned disjointedly to Kerr, glad of the darkness so that he couldn't see the way her eyes ate him up. He was so full of life and energy. She had been lucky; her hip would heal. But to ignore Colin's warning might be to see the life go out of this vital, handsome man.

'Who was that?' Kerr asked curtly as he reached her.

'Oh, just someone chatting about the view,' she lied, preparing to walk on, only Kerr had other ideas. His hand caught her already bruised wrist and she winced, coming to a halt.

'If you listen very carefully, you can hear the bells on the other leg ringing. You were talking to Ellis, weren't you?' he charged tersely.

Maxi stared at him. How could he possibly know? 'Don't be ridiculous,' she denied it with a laugh that was only a shade off key.

Kerr ground his teeth audibly. 'I don't call it being ridiculous to be suspicious when the emergency call I went back for turned out to be nothing of the sort. When it finally dawned on me that I was being kept talking, the question why was easily answered. To get you on your own. Who else could it be but Ellis? You thought you saw him today, and it would be too much of a coincidence for someone else to go to such lengths. I think it was Ellis, but if it wasn't, why are you so nervous, Maxi?'

And there she had it. If she continued to lie, then he would only become more suspicious, and she didn't need that. What she really needed was time to think, and nobody was giving it to her. 'All right, so it was Colin,' she admitted testily, getting her arm back and rubbing the bruised flesh gingerly. 'I didn't tell you because it seemed inappropriate.'

'What did he want?'

Maxi looked away, staring up at the night sky as if in search of inspiration. Her laugh carried an underlying bitterness. 'To talk over old times, of course.'

This time Kerr caught her by the shoulders and gave her a sharp shake. 'No man goes to those lengths just to talk over old times. What else did he want?' he demanded roughly, and she scowled at him, trying to think on her feet.

'Me. He wanted me, of course,' she goaded, shivering at the mere idea.

Kerr's eyes narrowed. 'Why now? Why after all this time?'

Oh, for goodness' sake, why couldn't he just drop it! 'He missed me!' she scoffed, and received another shake for her pains.

'Stop being so damned facetious! Just what are you trying to hide, Maxi?'

She winced, cursing herself for forgetting his incisive lawyer's brain. She knew she ought to tell him—after all, the main threat was against him—but until she had time to think, to consider all her options, she was reluctant to reveal the products of Colin's warped mind. It wasn't that she didn't value Kerr enough, but that she valued him too much. It scared her to think he might go in search of Colin, and she feared for his safety. Colin had no scruples, and she doubted if he went anywhere unarmed. She had to divert Kerr away from the danger somehow.

'Oh, Kerr, I'm not hiding anything,' she declared with a despairing sigh. 'Colin was just being himself, which is all the reason I need not to want to talk about him!'

A nerve began to jump in his jaw. 'There isn't much you do care to talk about, is there? Perhaps we should just stick to this!' he growled, and brought his mouth down on hers in a punishing kiss.

Instinctively she resisted him, although it was proving harder every time, and when she did manage to pull her mouth free she found herself looking up into glittering eyes. 'So, you don't want to do this either?' he scoffed, and about to agree, Maxi suddenly realised that here was her way, and one of his own instigation. She didn't hesitate.

With a wobbly sigh, she relaxed, allowing herself to lean lightly against him. 'You're wrong, I do want to,' she whispered huskily, tipping her head up, her bruised lips slightly parted invitingly.

The deep breath Kerr took was quite audible in the silent night. Maxi felt the tension in him as he brought his hands from her shoulders to rest lightly on her waist. 'No more games, Maxi?' he breathed against her lips, and she swallowed.

'No more games,' she agreed, although she had a sudden qualm that things might be going further than she had planned. Still she couldn't afford to back off now. Which was why she pressed her lips to his, using seductive strokes of her tongue to invite him to join her. He did, quite breathtakingly, making her skin tingle as her blood rushed recklessly through her veins.

Kerr's breath was moist and warm on her face when eventually they parted. 'So, you've finally stopped fighting me tooth and claw. Why tonight?'

Heart beating raggedly, Maxi pressed home her advantage. 'Because I'm so very tired of running. I changed my mind. That's a woman's prerogative. I can't help the timing, I only know I don't want to keep fighting you,

Kerr. You said I'd come to you in the end, and I have. Isn't that what you wanted to hear?' she challenged, voice sounding teasingly husky. Surely, when she was finally giving in, he wasn't going to refuse?

Kerr brought one hand up to lock in her hair, holding her face to what light came from the moon. 'It was,' he admitted slowly. 'Hell, it still is.'

Maxi tangled her fingers in the thick waves of hair at his nape and kept her eyes locked on his. 'I've always wanted you, you know that, Kerr. For once let's just be together without thinking.'

For one moment longer she thought he would refuse, but then she caught the gleam of his teeth as he smiled. 'Something tells me I should be arguing with you, but something stronger tells me to go for it before you change your mind again,' Kerr declared with rueful humour.

Maxi reached up on tiptoe to brush her lips over his. 'I won't do that,' she breathed.

Kerr's eyes seemed to bore into hers. 'No, I don't believe you would,' he agreed at last. 'You're a strong woman, Maxine Ambro, prepared to make decisions and keep to them. It would take a lot to make you change your mind, wouldn't it?'

Confident that the dangerous moment had passed, she laughed huskily. 'Is that a crime?' she teased, and he shook his head.

'No. But it does make what we're about to do very interesting. Let's go,' he declared, and, slipping an arm about her shoulders, urged her back the way they had come.

As she went with him, Maxi couldn't quite shake off the nagging feeling that command of the situation had somehow escaped her grasp. Yet he was only doing what she had wanted him to do. He had forgotten about Colin, at least temporarily, and she couldn't be sorry that it had taken the abandonment of her stance to do it.

There was a strong smell of paint in the air as Kerr let them inside his house half an hour later. Fliss and Andy had come in their own car, so Kerr had taken the direct route home.

Going ahead of her, Kerr switched on the lounge light, then uncovered the cocktail trolley. 'Would you like something to drink?'

Maxi shook her head, too nervous suddenly to want to add spirits to her bloodstream. 'You have one if you like.'

He came back to her. 'I'll pass, too. There wouldn't be any fun in either of us being in too much of an alcoholic mist to enjoy ourselves,' he teased softly. Sliding his hands around her waist, he pulled her close, searching her face for any sign of wavering. 'Still sure this is what you want?'

Maxi couldn't blame him for being suspicious, when she had held out for so long. She knew her smile was tense, but it was a tension due to anticipation, not doubt. That indescribable chemistry was already beginning to set her pulses thrumming. Whatever the reason for her change of mind, she knew she had nothing to fear from him. 'I've never been more sure. Make love to me, Kerr. I want you to.'

Was there a man alive who would need more urging than that? Certainly not Kerr. Her words had fanned a flame in his eye, and he brought his head down to hers with a throaty growl of triumph. 'God, how I've hungered for you!' he breathed against her lips, and then he was kissing her with a leashed passion that wiped her mind clean, leaving her only able to respond with an equal passion of her own.

To be free at last to abandon her defences sent a shivering wave of delight through her. This was everything and more than she had ever expected. Tiny little explosions of pleasure were going off inside her as the world shrank to encompass only the two of them. When he broke the kiss to sweep her up into his arms, they were both breathing erratically. The heat of passion lay on his cheekbones, telling her, had she not already known it, just how much he wanted her. The hot lance of his eyes turned her insides molten, and she knew that if he hadn't been holding her she would have crumpled to the floor. She folded her arms about his neck, and her fingers locked into his hair as she closed her eyes and let him carry her up the stairs to his room.

Unlike all the others, the dust covers here had been removed, and the bed made. Setting her on her feet beside it, Kerr switched on the bedside lamp, bathing the room in a soft golden glow. He turned back to her then, framing her head in strong yet gentle hands. 'I've dreamt of having you here,' he growled with a husky laugh, taking her lips again, bruising them with nips of his teeth, then soothing the hurt with erotic strokes of his tongue.

Maxi tried to hang on to her spinning senses, reaching out to fumble with the buttons of his shirt. She wanted to touch him, had ached to do so for so long that she trembled, her body quickening with a hot rush of desire. Pushing the shirt from his shoulders, she groaned aloud as she allowed her hands to search out the planes of his hair-roughened chest. She had never known such pleasure could be possible from just touching a man's body. Pleasure was an unknown quantity to her, and she had waited so long to experience it that she felt quite dizzy. Then Kerr caught his breath as her questing fingers found his flat male nipples, and brought his hands up to stay her.

'You're sending me up in flames, and I want this to last, to be special,' he growled pushing her hands to her sides. 'It's my turn.' Gently he eased open the buttons of her blouse, tossing it aside as he revealed the wisp of lacy bra beneath. Maxi held her breath as he deftly released the catch and freed her breasts to his burning gaze.

They peaked, sending a *frisson* of pleasure along her nerves.

'You're beautiful,' he declared throatily, unzipping her trousers and pushing them down over her hips so that they fell to the floor.

She stood revealed to him then, only a small wisp of lace remaining to cover her. To see the wanting in him, to know it was mirrored in herself, made her feel proud of her femininity. She felt fresh and clean, as if this was the first time. And truly it was, the first time with an equal desire, if not with an equal love. In that moment she didn't care what her eyes revealed, only that he made her feel beautiful, able to respond naturally, not with the pretence that Colin had forced upon her.

'I knew you could make me feel this,' she admitted honestly, and cast herself into his arms, clinging to him as she rained kisses over his face, caressing him boldly so that he moaned in her arms before lifting her on to the bed and coming down on top of her.

It was a weight she welcomed, until his angry voice growled in her ear. 'And you knew you could make me feel the same, didn't you? That's what you were banking on.' Coming up on his elbows, his grey eyes revealed the same anger as she reluctantly focused on him. 'Damn you, Maxi, I never thought you'd really go this far just to stop me asking questions about Ellis!'

The heat died out of her rapidly as she realised she hadn't fooled him at all. Throat working madly, she turned her head away. 'Let me go!' she ordered gruffly.

'Not until you talk to me,' Kerr countered swiftly. 'What else happened out there on the Cobb? What was it he said that you'd go this far to stop me knowing?'

When she remained stubbornly mute, Kerr rolled off her, but only on to his knees, from where he dragged her up into a sitting position. Feeling more defeated than she ever had in her life before, she squeezed her eyes shut.

'He threatened you,' she finally answered in a tone barely above a whisper.

'What was that?' Kerr charged sharply, and, goaded by the knowledge of her own foolishness, her head came up, eyes flashing sparks at him.

'He threatened you!' she cried. 'He wants me back, and he warned me not to go to the police! There, are you satisfied now?'

Sheer surprise made his hold slacken, and she took advantage of it to slide off the side of the bed, reaching for her blouse. Kerr recovered quickly, though, coming up beside her.

'No, I'm damn well not satisfied. What do you mean, threatened me? How? With what?' he barked the question at her.

Struggling into her clothes with jerky movements, Maxi laughed humourlessly. 'Your life, by any method he cares to think of,' she retorted unevenly, and looked at him when he swore. 'Don't worry, I'm not about to let him hurt you or anyone else.'

Kerr was clearly staggered. Watching her fasten buttons, he dragged a hand through his hair. 'Hold on—you're saying you were protecting me? Why?'

That was coming too close to the truth, and she hoisted her chin defiantly. 'I don't know. I'm just crazy, I guess.'

He swore again, more succinctly. 'For sure, one of us is crazy. Just how were you planning to stop him?'

That deflated her again, and she bit her lip, frowning. 'I don't know. I've got to think about it.'

At that Kerr moved swiftly to stand in front of her. 'Oh, no, if anyone is going to think of something, then it's me.'

Which was what she was afraid of. 'Don't be a fool, he's dangerous.'

'And you're a woman!'

Dressed at last, Maxi wanted nothing more than to leave, but she couldn't let that pass. 'A woman who can look after herself.'

Grey eyes narrowed consideringly. 'That sounds like the voice of experience speaking. What else aren't you going to tell me, Maxi?' When she refused to answer, he smiled menacingly. 'You know, I could take you back to bed and make you tell me.'

She gasped. 'Only an utter bastard would even try it!'

He laughed. 'But I am a bastard, as you've told me more than once. So why were you so concerned I might get hurt?'

Having been backed so neatly into a corner, the only thing to do was come out fighting. 'Right this minute, for the life of me I couldn't tell you!'

Kerr studied her for a long time in silence, then reached for his shirt. 'OK, I'll leave it for now. Give me a minute to dress and I'll drive us home. But don't imagine I'll forget—you'll tell me everything I want to know in the end. As for Ellis's threat, you aren't handling it on your own, and that's final. It's my life, Maxi, and nobody uses me to get to you. Whatever you may have had to do in the past, we're doing this together.'

# CHAPTER NINE

HAVING fallen asleep last night when she hadn't thought she would, Maxi overslept in the morning, and washed and dressed in a hurry. Not bothering with make-up, she was still tucking her shirt into her jeans as she descended the stairs. There was only one question in her mind: where was Kerr? Last night, having forced the truth out of her, he had said they would work together, but she didn't trust him not to go off and do something on his own. The thought of the consequences had her chewing anxiously at her lip when she went through to the breakfast-room.

Nor was her anxiety allayed when she found only her mother there, lingering over her coffee as she read the newspaper.

'Good morning, darling. Did you sleep well?' her mother asked, watching as Maxi helped herself to coffee and nothing else. 'I do wish you'd eat more.'

Maxi felt so nervy that she'd have trouble just swallowing a liquid right then. 'I'm not hungry, really,' she protested faintly, taking a much needed sip of coffee.

'You can't be worried about your weight,' Lady Ambro protested, laying aside her newspaper. 'You used to eat like a horse and never put on a pound.'

Forcing a laugh, Maxi drained her cup. 'I still do, but not in the morning.' She glanced at her watch. It was already well past nine o'clock. 'Er—where's Kerr? Have you seen him this morning?' she asked, trying to make the question sound idle, and not the urgent one it actually was.

'He was here earlier. I believe he went to have a word with your father in his study.'

Which, while it eased her mind one way, only raised further questions. What were they talking about? As it happened, she didn't have to wait long to find out. There was no advance warning, just the sudden opening of the door to let Kerr, closely followed by her father, into the room.

For a reason she couldn't explain, Maxi held her breath, knowing only that with their entrance an energy field seemed to have entered the room, too. The air seemed to seethe with a volatile mixture of emotions. Her father, looking vaguely ill at ease, failed to meet her eyes as he went to his wife's side, while Kerr looked positively grim. He stalked—there was no other word to describe it—to her chair, breathing so heavily that Maxi had the slightly hysterical thought he was in danger of busting his shirt buttons.

'Where's Fliss?' He barked the question so sharply that he made everyone jump.

'W-why, she's at the tennis court,' Lady Ambro divulged nervously, all at sea, glancing up at her husband when he laid a calming hand on her shoulder.

Having apparently heard all he needed to know, Kerr manacled Maxi's wrist in a grip that stopped the flow of blood and jerked her bodily to her feet. 'Excuse us. We have some...business...to discuss,' he declared ominously and dragged her away.

It was not the sort of treatment Maxi was prepared to take lying down, but she waited until they were well out of earshot before putting on the brakes and trying to prise his fingers off. 'Have you gone mad? Let me go this instant!'

It was a paltry attempt that hardly caused him to break his stride. He merely gave her arm a yank and carried on his way. 'I'll let you go when I'm good and ready, Maxine Ambro. And if, for once in your misbegotten life, you keep quiet, I won't chuck you in the pool as we go by! Tempting though the thought undoubtedly is!' he hissed through his teeth.

She remained silent only because words were jammed in her throat. However, her exhalations of breath were vocal enough of her fury, and Kerr had no trouble at all in interpreting them.

'Stop spitting, little cat, or so help me...!' He didn't need to enlarge on the warning; she got the message. This was trouble with a capital T, and she only hoped he would explain and give her a chance to form some sort of defence. She didn't have long to wait.

'I've just had a very illuminating talk with your father,' he went on conversationally, and Maxi's heart leapt up to increase the blockage in her throat. Kerr cast a swift glance at her, lips mockingly curved. 'What, nothing to say? Wonders will never cease! John seemed to think that as you and I were "getting along" as he so tactfully put it, then you must have told me.'

Although she thought she knew, still the words came out in an automatic delaying action. 'Told you what?'

In the quiet garden, it was possible to hear his teeth grate—almost. 'How can you sound so innocent? I'm referring to what we both know you haven't said one damn word about, Maxi! I don't know it all, because I decided not to add to your father's concern, but I'm going to. There's been enough stupidity around here. It's time everyone, and I mean *everyone*, knew the truth!'

Now she did manage to find her voice, and, because the pool was only a step away, decided that discretion was the better part of valour. To continue pretending ignorance would only get her an unwanted ducking. 'That *was* my intention when I came here. However, you might just have noticed Fliss's reluctance to listen. And as for telling you...' She allowed that to tail off eloquently.

Kerr uttered a bark of mirthless laughter. 'You didn't think I had the right to know, because you couldn't care less what I thought of you?' he guessed accurately.

Accurate, that was, up to a point. Now it mattered, now that she knew just who he was and what she felt for him. 'Something like that.'

'They say you learn a little something every day, and whoever "they" are, they're right. That's quite a complex you've got. Enjoy playing the martyr, do you?' he jeered, and her temper flared because it wasn't like that at all. Sometimes he made her so damn mad, she could spit nails!

'Go to hell!'

They had, by this time, reached the fenced-off tennis court, and Kerr fumbled with the gate. 'I've been there, thanks, and frankly it's underrated. Hi, there!' He raised his voice as Fliss, hearing their approach, turned from where she had been practising shots with the aid of a machine.

'Hi,' she greeted, giving her sister a reserved smile, before looking curiously at the way Kerr was holding Maxi's wrist. Her brows rose. 'Is something wrong?'

'Yes!'

'No.'

They spoke together, but a speaking look from Kerr won him the advantage. 'Maxi has something she wants to tell you,' he declared in the kind of voice teachers used when they wanted you to admit to a misdemeanour.

Fliss frowned, looked hard at Kerr, and, to the surprise of them both, set her jaw. 'Maxi doesn't have to tell me anything she doesn't want to.'

Maxi felt her heart swell with emotion. For the first time in seven long years, Fliss was actually being protective instead of condemning. It made a whole world of difference. 'No, Kerr's right. There's something I've wanted to tell you for a long time,' she admitted gruffly.

Fliss picked at the gut of her racket. 'About Colin.' It was a statement, not a question, and she sighed shakily. 'Perhaps we ought to sit down.'

They sat side by side on the bench. Kerr, having released his hold on Maxi, leant against the wire fencing, legs and arms crossed in an attitude of relaxation that his watchful expression belied.

Maxi sought for the right words. 'What I have to say may shock you, Fliss, but please, hear me out before you say anything.' Hands clenched into fists, she took a deep breath. 'Did it ever occur to you to wonder why, seven years ago, I took Colin away from you the way I did? We could simply have left, but I wanted you to hate him, and was prepared for you to hate me too, because I knew he never wanted you. He was obsessed with me, Fliss, but I never encouraged him, and I never thought he would use you to get to me. I never liked him, but I disliked him even more after that. When I came home and found out, I broke it up as soon as I could because I wanted to stop him from ruining your life.

'I know that sounds hopelessly melodramatic, but I was afraid, because there were things about him you didn't know, and at the time I could only guess at. Oh, Fliss, when I couldn't get through to you, I was in despair. I couldn't get you to see that Colin was two-faced. He looked mild, but he had a violent temper. He didn't look as if he took drugs, but he did. He liked to make conquests, and boast about them. I came to understand later that what he liked best of all was to corrupt.

'Anyway, at the time, I knew that he never planned to marry you, Fliss. I went to Father, but he thought I was just jealous. Then I tried the police, but I had no proof of anything illegal. That's when I decided that I had to take him away, but I had to make sure you'd hate him enough never to take him back. If that sounds like a martyr to anyone, I'm not about to apologise. I loved you too much to see you hurt.'

The end of her story fell into a pool of silence. All that could be heard was the rhythmic sound of the machine serving balls over the net, and then even that stopped as it was emptied. For a while nobody spoke, but Maxi was intensely conscious of Kerr's presence behind her. Then suddenly Fliss jumped to her feet, hands wringing the racket handle.

'I've been such a fool!' she wailed.

'You were very young,' Maxi ameliorated gently, only to have her sister utter a groan.

'Not then, now! Oh, Maxi, I've treated you so badly since you arrived, and I haven't even got Colin for an excuse!'

Maxi looked justifiably confused. 'I don't understand.'

Fliss's face was a picture of contrition. 'I knew Colin was wrong for me years ago. The minute I met Andy, I knew. I always meant to tell you, but I was such a coward. Then, when you came back, you were so happy for me, and I just felt even guiltier. I over-reacted. Andy was so furious with me, but I just couldn't seem to help it. Everything I said came out worse and worse. Everyone liked you, and forgave you, and I was so green with jealousy! I always thought I came second best when you were around.'

Maxi was on her feet at once. 'Oh, Fliss, that's just not true. We all love you,' she declared huskily, and, when her sister burst into tears, took her in her arms.

'I know,' Fliss sobbed in a wobbly voice. 'I hated myself. Especially for using Kerr against you when it's obvious how much you like each other. I'm really sorry. Can you forgive me?'

'Only if you forgive me,' Maxi countered, near to tears herself.

'I do, I do!' Fliss insisted, pulling free and wiping her eyes, and the pair of them grinned at each other in an excess of relief. Until Fliss abruptly sobered again. 'But,

Maxi, if you didn't even like Colin, why did you marry him?'

She hadn't expected the question, and, even though she had told Fliss practically everything, there were still some things that were too private and personal. Smiling ruefully, Maxi shrugged and sat down again. 'I didn't mean to, it just sort of happened. Perhaps I thought I could change him, you know, like a good woman is supposed to do. Anyway, it didn't work, so I ended it as soon as I could.'

However, Fliss, having shucked off her childish jealousy, wasn't about to leave it at that. Face mirroring her concern, she sat down beside her sister. 'You said he had a violent temper. He didn't hurt you, did he?'

Trust Fliss to cut through the gloss, Maxi thought wryly, and spread her hands wide. 'Do I look as though I suffered? Besides, there wasn't time—the marriage only lasted for six months, seven years ago. It wasn't a picnic, but I've put it well and truly behind me.'

'Are you telling me the truth?' Fliss questioned determinedly, like a dog with a bone. 'I couldn't bear to think of anything happening to you because of me.'

Maxi laughed. 'May the ground open and swallow me up if I tell a lie!' she declared, using the oath of their childhood.

Fliss grinned, immediately relaxing. 'Golly, I feel as if I'm floating on air. I've felt so miserable for days. I'm sorry I didn't listen to you back then, Maxi, and I'm glad we've cleared the air at last. It means we're really a family again, just in time for the wedding.' She sat up straight almost immediately. 'I've got to go and tell Andy the good news. Are you coming?'

Maxi was on the point of agreeing when she felt two strong hands come down on her shoulders. 'We'll be along later,' Kerr answered for them.

'OK.' With an effervescence that had been lacking of late, Fliss kissed them both, grabbed up her racket and ran off.

A silence fell about them then, so deep that Maxi could quite clearly hear the buzzing of bees and the clicking of crickets. But only peripherally, for her attention was focused on the man behind her.

'Don't you want to know if I forgive you, too?' Kerr's voice spoke almost directly into her ear, making her jump, and sending shivers down her spine.

Of course she did. What human being would actively choose to have people hate them? But... 'It won't make any difference if you do or not.'

'I could have won a fortune on betting you'd say that. However, it might not make a difference to you, but to me it does. You put on a very convincing show seven years ago, but I'm glad to know it was only a show.'

Her leaping nerves told her the conversation was taking an unexpected turn. Not clear where it was taking her, she felt her way carefully. 'My marriage was a very real one,' she pointed out, unable to keep the edge from her voice. Immediately she felt his hands lift, but only to allow him to move round to straddle the bench. Head tipped to one side as he studied her.

'I'd be interested to hear about that marriage of yours, Maxi. Without the precautionary crossing of your fingers behind your back,' he mused drily, watching the colour storm into her cheeks.

She could kick herself for having forgotten he was behind her when she used that childish trick. All she could do was stare him out. 'My marriage is over. I'm not about to do a post-mortem on it now.'

'The results could be very revealing.'

That was what she was afraid of, and it propelled her to her feet. 'I know all about it. I was there. Now all I want to do is forget it ever happened.'

Kerr's hand shot out to foil her attempt to leave. 'Can you, though? Somehow I doubt it. Dammit, don't close up on me!' This as he saw her lashes flutter down. 'My God, must you always shut everyone out? You may have had to fight your own battles before, but you're not alone any more. Let someone else take part of the burden. I'm not your father or your sister. I don't need the truth diluted. Stop trying to protect everyone and let them protect you for a change. Tell the whole truth for once. Did the bastard hurt you?'

His anger rolled across her in waves, only it wasn't directed at her, but at Colin. Yet that didn't surprise her so much as the sheer intensity of his anger. There was a wildness in his eyes, too, which seemed to suggest the answer mattered to him, but she couldn't understand why, when she knew for a fact he didn't love her—which was enough to bring her chin up.

'Whatever the truth is or isn't, what's it to you? Why should I tell anything to a man who's made it very plain he despises me?'

At that Kerr gave a bark of mocking laughter. 'Hell, you're right. How can I expect you to see, when I've been criminally blind myself? You have every right not to trust me, Maxi, but nevertheless I'm telling you that you can. As for despising you, if it seemed as if I did, then I'm a better actor than I thought. Right now I'm too busy despising myself. *Tell* me. I need to know just what kind of man he is in order to deal with him. So I'll ask you one more time, did he hurt you?'

It was hard to think of Colin when his declaration that he didn't despise her was echoing back and forth in her brain. Even though she longed to talk to someone, she couldn't drop all her defences. 'He never put me in hospital, if that's what you want to know,' she admitted brusquely, and heard the hissing intake of his breath.

'Meaning he never hit you, or that the results weren't enough for hospitalisation?' he gritted out painfully, and her eyes flew to his, seeing his anger...and his pain.

Unable to look away, she swallowed hard. 'The latter,' she acknowledged huskily, and watched as her answer brought forth a torrent of muttered oaths.

Abruptly Kerr rose to his full height, walking over to the wire fence and hitting it with a violence that made her gasp and must have hurt him. 'If I ever get close to the bastard, I'll kill him with my bare hands, so help me God!'

Maxi's throat closed over, and she didn't dare begin to imagine what that explosive anger meant, choosing instead to go to him, taking his hand in hers and examining it. There was bleeding from several grazes, and she quickly produced a handkerchief and used it as a makeshift bandage. Only then did she look up at him in a kind of daze.

But before she could ask the burning question, Kerr sent her a grim look. 'Tell me about it, Maxi, before I go insane with wondering.'

She didn't understand, but she nodded slowly, eyes never leaving his. 'OK. It's quite a long story, so we'd better sit down.'

When they were once more sitting side by side, she cleared her throat, finding it difficult to know where to start. 'I suppose the real beginning was when I married Colin. I told Fliss the truth when I said I hadn't intended to; what I didn't say was that he virtually blackmailed me into it. He made a veiled threat about her, and told me he'd deny it if I went to the police. Well, I'd already discovered they couldn't help me, so I agreed. At the time, I didn't really think he was dangerous, although I guessed he took drugs. Oh, I had some crazy idea that I could marry him under my own rules. I certainly didn't intend to sleep with him. I thought I could prove it wouldn't work, and then get a divorce.'

'But it wasn't like that?' Kerr encouraged, when her words tailed off into painful memories.

'No,' she agreed with a harsh laugh. 'My instinct not to like him was well founded. Once he had his ring on my finger, he revealed himself in his true colours. He had a violent temper, and he didn't like to be thwarted. From the start I wasn't allowed to sleep alone, and the fact that I wouldn't respond to him angered him.' Maxi paused then, licking dry lips as she recalled that first crisis point. When she went on, her voice was husky. 'I'd never experienced violence before, and I don't mind admitting that he scared me. The second time he slapped me around because of my "frigidity", I decided the best thing to do was pretend. I was very convincing. I…made all the right noises, all the right moves, and that pleased him. He decided he wanted it to go on. I became very good at faking pleasure.'

Kerr caught his breath, and his voice was gravelly when he asked, 'Why didn't you leave him? Surely you didn't feel any loyalty for the creep?'

'No, I didn't. I loathed him. I could have gone after the first few weeks, and I would have, but two things happened. There was one particular time, when he was high, that I did or said something he didn't like, and he beat me up quite badly.' The memory made her eyes burn with a fierce hatred, even when her lips curved in a chilling smile. 'It was a kind of poetic justice, because I couldn't work. I stayed at home, and that was how I discovered that he wasn't just taking drugs, he was importing them and dealing too.'

By this time Kerr was frowning heavily, following every word with a deep concentration. 'You're saying that made you stay?'

'Yes,' she agreed, with a fierce delight. 'I discovered I didn't just want to walk away. I wanted to get him put away for the misery he was causing thousands of people, not just me. I wanted that more than my freedom. I wanted them to lock him up and throw away the key! So I went to the DEA and offered to help them get him.'

'Good God! Didn't you think of the danger?' Kerr exclaimed, taking her by the shoulders and staring into her emotive face. 'For God's sake, Maxi, you could have been killed!' There was a wealth of pent-up agony in that exclamation, and, when she actually looked into his grey eyes and saw the alarm there, the fever went out of her, and she sighed apologetically.

'Of course I did. But I've never backed away from what I knew was right. I *had* to do it. It took several months, but with my help they caught him. I was in court to hear him sentenced, then I left and went straight out and got myself a divorce. That was the greatest day of my life! I felt as if I'd been released from prison.'

There, it was out at last, and she experienced a wave of relief, as if a great weight had been lifted off her shoulders. She hadn't realised just how heavy a burden her unspoken memories had been. But what did Kerr make of it all?

When she looked up at him, he was rubbing his hands over his face. 'So all the time I thought you were gallivanting with Fliss's man, you were actually conspiring to put him in gaol. Why didn't you tell anyone?'

She raised a shoulder diffidently. 'It wasn't the sort of thing I could write home about. Unfortunately they didn't throw away the key. He got out much sooner than I ever expected.'

'And now he's back to get his revenge by threatening me,' Kerr guessed accurately. 'How does he intend to take it?'

She shivered, recalled to the far more dangerous present. Immediately Kerr reached across to take her hand in his much larger one, and she glanced up to see such a look of blinding fury in his eyes that her heart stopped. 'He said he wants me back, and that you could have an accident just like mine if I refused, or went to the police.'

'The man's certifiable. I'm sure that piece of information will be of great interest to our detective, because, if I'm not very much mistaken, we now know the identity of your burglar. Who else hates you enough to trash your flat?' Kerr fell silent then, for a long time, eventually turning to her with a frown. 'Obviously you haven't said yes, so he's going to have to contact you again. Do you know when?'

'He's going to ring me here at noon,' she told him quickly, and he glanced at his watch.

'Ten-thirty. That means we have an hour and a half to come up with an idea. I'm going to ring that detective, and our local police. Between us we should be able to plan a suitable reception for Ellis. One to teach him he threatens you at his peril,' Kerr declared grimly, getting to his feet once more.

Maxi rose too, feeling rather wobbly inside at the way he had made that last statement. Good lord, it almost sounded as if he cared! Not daring to let her hopes take wing, she frowned up at him.

'Why are you doing this, Kerr? Why are you helping me?' she wanted to know. He looked at her as if he had forgotten she was there, and then, to her amazement, a slow flush rose into his cheeks.

'Darling, you may be brave and foolhardy, but you are also incredibly dense. Unfortunately we don't have the time to discuss it right now. It would take too long, and I don't intend to do it less than justice. But if you need a clue...'

In the blink of an eye Maxi found herself swept into a hard embrace and had the breath kissed out of her. It ended much too soon, and she was given no time to ask all the million and one questions that bubbled inside her, for Kerr urged her trembling legs back towards the house.

She didn't have the strength to protest, and wouldn't have anyway. Because suddenly the man she had thought was her enemy was now her ally, and that opened the door to the sort of miracle she hadn't dared hope for.

# CHAPTER TEN

MAXI was unaware how extremely chic she looked in her lightweight peach silk suit, and Kerr, who sat opposite her in the bow-window of one of the quaint tearooms in Lyme Regis, only registered it marginally himself.

'What time is it?' she asked huskily.

'A quarter to two. I'll have to be going. We need to be in place well in advance,' Kerr told her shortly, as if daring her to argue.

Maxi ignored the warning. 'I wish you'd change your mind and stay here.'

He smiled grimly, for they had been over this many times. 'You're not going out to face him alone.'

She glared at him. Why couldn't he see she was worried he might get hurt? 'I won't be alone. The police will be there,' she pointed out again.

'I don't care if they are there!' he began explosively, then hastily moderated his tone when heads turned. 'You could have a whole damn army with you, but I won't be satisfied unless I'm there too!' he finished through his teeth.

Lord, he could be so damn stubborn, she thought, smiling wryly. 'And, of course, you'll make all the difference!'

Now his smile was genuine as he reached across to cuff her chin gently with his fist. 'You'd better believe it.'

Aware, as she had been for some hours, of a vital change in their relationship, Maxi sighed. 'Then you'd better be going.'

Nodding, Kerr rose to his feet, but had taken no more than a couple of steps before he swung back to her, and, uncaring of their audience, bent and pressed a hard kiss on her surprised mouth. 'Take care,' he ordered gruffly, and this time made good his departure.

She watched his progress until he went from her view, her smile fading then as a chill of apprehension raced along her spine. Time seemed to be going exceedingly slow now the hour approached, whereas the time before noon had been a blur of activity. Kerr had spoken to her father, and then the pair of them had spent ages on the telephone. Apparently Colin's fingerprints had already been matched to those found in her flat, and this, with what she had to add, caused the constabulary to move with dizzying speed.

Kerr had been amazingly supportive, insisting on being with her when she took Colin's call at precisely twelve o'clock. The arrangements had been simple. She had told him she would meet him on the Cobb at two-thirty, and would give him her answer then. She had imagined he would argue, but he hadn't, and then she had recalled his supreme confidence. He already thought he had won.

That would give them the edge they needed, she decided as she paid her bill and left. Ahead of her the Cobb stretched out its mighty arm into the sparkling sea. Out there, somewhere, was her ex-husband. But out there, too, was Kerr and any number of police, and that gave her the boost of adrenalin needed to face her tormentor for the last time. At the foot of the groyne she halted, searching for that familiar figure among the many sightseers. But she was unable to pick him out and slowly began to walk out along the top.

There were fewer people towards the end, and she could see those that arrived and departed by the steps to the lower level. Right at the very end, two fishermen were busy baiting their rods, and between them and herself a few couples strolled along, some with their children dancing about their legs. But there was no single man. Maxi stopped, glancing round, wondering what to do next. A childless couple were turning back. They smiled at her as they passed.

'You came, then,' a voice stated behind her, and she swung round, startled. There must have been more than one set of steps from the lower level, for Colin had appeared out of nowhere.

'You knew I would,' she said coldly, noticing that his once dapper appearance now looked very slightly seedy.

Colin smiled unpleasantly. 'You must love him very much.'

'I always did, and I always will, but that isn't what we came here to talk about,' Maxi stated evenly, knowing from past experience that it was important to remain in control. Colin fed off other people's emotions as a parasite lived off its host.

His face turned nasty. 'You always were a cold little bitch.'

Maxi swallowed hard on a wave of bile. Looking beyond him, she noticed that the fishermen had given up and were walking towards them. Were they police? She didn't know; her only instructions were to keep Colin talking as long as possible. 'Only towards you. I'll always despise you, so why don't you just let me go?'

'No can do, love, sorry. You don't get off that easily. Life wasn't pleasant for me inside, and now it won't be for you. Let's go.' He stepped forward to take her by the arm, and in the same instance all hell broke loose.

Suddenly there were people everywhere. Colin cried out as the two fishermen pounced on him from behind. Realising he had been tricked, he put up a furious fight, managing to break free for a few vital seconds. He came straight for her, and although another man executed a perfect rugby tackle, it brought Colin crashing into her. She felt herself staggering and falling, then the ground seemed to disappear from under her, and with a piercing scream she tumbled over the side.

Yet almost in that same instant, a vice clamped about her wrist almost jarring her arm from its socket, and instead of falling into the sea below, she crashed into the stonework and hung there, winded. Then miraculously she heard Kerr's voice telling her she was all right, that he had her, and very slowly she began to be hauled upwards.

She hadn't even realised she was crying until she collapsed into his arms when she was once more safe on terra firma. She clung on like grim death as the reality that she had been saved from a potentially fatal accident, and by none less than Kerr himself. Finally, when her nerves had settled somewhat, she pushed herself away a little, wiping moisture from her eyes.

'You were right, you did make the difference,' she told him gruffly.

'You'd better believe it,' he repeated shakily, before taking time out to study her. 'How do you feel? I'm afraid your stockings are ruined.'

Relief made her feel quite heady. 'I'd sacrifice any number of pairs, so long as you're there to catch me when I fall!' she gasped, sobering very slowly, and finding herself staring into fathomless grey eyes which appeared to be inviting her to drown in them.

Before either could say anything, though, they were interrupted. 'Is she OK? Sorry we couldn't hold on to him a bit better.'

Maxi looked up swiftly, responding to the reassuring smile of the young woman who had passed her. She was obviously part of the force, as was her partner, who was now adding his weight to that of the other two men. From a distance she heard one fisherman cautioning Colin while the young man slipped on handcuffs.

'I'm fine, really. Just a couple of scraped knees,' she reassured the woman, deciding not to mention the near dislocated arm, plus a body which was already bruising, and would no doubt ache like the devil tomorrow.

Kerr dragged a none-too-steady hand through his hair. 'All the same, I want to get you home,' he said decisively, and started when a hand clamped on his shoulder.

'Well done, Mr Devereaux, it worked like a dream,' the fisherman said, then nodded to Maxi. 'DS Short, Miss Ambro. You can relax now, we've got the ... so-and-so. So if you'll both come back to the station with us, we can book laddie here and take statements.' He glanced round at the considerable crowd they'd attracted. 'If we stay here any longer, they'll think we're a sideshow.'

It was a further two hours before they were finally free to go. By that time her body was already beginning to protest in reaction to her fall. Kerr took one look at her pale, strained face, and told her to stay where she was while he went to bring the car round to the front of the police station. Once in the car, she sat back with a sigh and closed her eyes.

'Where are we going?' she asked tiredly, not really caring, just glad it was all over.

'Back to my place,' Kerr informed her, without taking his eyes off the road. 'What you need is a long soak in a hot bath.'

She couldn't argue with that; in fact it sounded wonderful. Still she chose to prevaricate a little, lest he think he was going to have everything his own way. 'I could do that at my parents' place.'

Kerr's lips curved upwards. 'I know, but if you think I'm going to let you out of my sight you're mistaken. You and I still have a lot of things to sort out—that's why we're going to my house.'

Her eyes came open as her head turned, and she studied his profile lazily. 'What things?'

'Oh, important things. Such as—do you love me, Maxi?' he declared in a voice which wasn't quite as casual as he tried to make it.

She was taken by surprise, although in truth she shouldn't see why she was when she must have betrayed herself any number of ways in the last twenty-four hours. Yet for him to come out and boldly ask her, and in a tone which seemed to suggest her answer was important, made her hold back a pride-saving evasion. Should she hesitate? Wasn't there a point where a gamble was worth the risk?

'You must know that I do,' she admitted huskily, deciding there was.

Kerr's soft laugh had a ragged edge to it, and his chest swelled as he took a deep breath. 'I heard you tell Ellis you did, but I couldn't be sure it wasn't just fighting talk.'

Maxi swallowed hard to hide her disappointment that he hadn't returned the compliment. 'There are some things I would never lie about.'

'That's what I thought, so it's only fair to tell you that I love you, too.'

Even though she'd heard it, she could scarcely believe he'd really said it. After all their fighting, it just seemed so incredible. 'Kerr!' she exclaimed, sitting up straighter. 'How . . . when?'

He sent her a brief but intense look which halted the stumbling flow. 'All in good time. First things first. You need that bath. There will be plenty of time to talk later.'

Although she was bursting to have all her questions answered, she subsided, feeling her heart swelling with a happiness she had thought lost forever seven years ago. With a childish gesture, she actually pinched herself to make sure it was real, that she hadn't fallen asleep and was dreaming. But it was real all right, and she spent the rest of the journey with her eyes fastened on his strong profile.

At last the house loomed up, but before she could do more than unfasten her seatbelt Kerr was round the car and opening her door, picking her up in his arms. It felt so good to be held by him that Maxi wasn't even tempted to protest. He carried her right up to his bedroom, and through to the bathroom, only setting her on her feet then so that he could start running water into the bath.

Looking on in a pleasant daze, Maxi took the large fluffy towels he produced from the cupboard. 'Take all the time you need,' he advised her. 'Do you need any help?'

She was tempted to say yes, but shook her head anyway. 'I can manage.'

He smiled wryly. 'Hmm, just my luck. Don't lock the door, and shout if you need anything.'

When he had gone, she quickly pulled herself together. Finding some bath salts on a shelf, she added a liberal amount before shedding her clothes and sinking gratefully into the water. It was sheer bliss, and she felt the warmth begin to work on her strained muscles. Sighing, she let her thoughts drift away, only to have them rudely interrupted when she heard the door open.

'I've brought you that drink you refused last night,' he informed her, looking amused by the frantic attempts she was making to cover herself with the inadequate sponge.

Deciding it was a wasted effort, she abandoned the attempt, and accepted the glass with all the aplomb she could manage. 'Thank you.'

Grey eyes danced. 'You're welcome. I'll take your clothes and find you something else to wear.' At the door, he glanced back. 'Don't fall asleep and drown, will you? I wouldn't want to lose you so soon.'

She caught her breath. 'You plan on keeping me, then?'

Kerr sobered a little. 'If you want to stay.'

Maxi glanced down into the golden brandy. So, he still had doubts that she might leave. She liked that—it meant he was taking nothing for granted. 'You'll have to convince me it would be worth my while,' she told him huskily, and immediately his smile returned with confidence.

'Oh, I intend to,' he promised, and once more left her alone.

Maxi sipped at her drink, a cat-like smile curving her lips. Her visit home hadn't turned out the way she had expected at all. She had had to fight all the way, but she was glad she'd done it, because now she knew the greatest prize of all was within her grasp.

When she walked out of the bathroom almost an hour later, swathed in an enormous bath sheet, she came to an abrupt halt. Laid out carefully on the bed was a dress—a plain ivory silk shift beneath a chiffon over-dress that would fall in gentle folds to just above her knees. But not only that, there were shoes and underwear, too, and standing by the dresser was her own make-up case. She was still staring at it all in astonishment, when Kerr walked in.

'Oh good, you're out. I was just coming to tell you it was getting late,' he declared offhandedly, increasing her confusion.

'Getting late for what? And what is all this?' she cast an arm over the laden bed.

'They're not my size, so they must be for you,' he quipped as he disappeared into his dressing-room, emerging a minute or two later with an armful of clothes. 'I rang Fliss and asked her to bring something over, as your clothes were ruined. You're much of a size, so they should fit.'

Feeling weak, Maxi sank down on to the edge of the bed. 'I don't understand. What's going on?'

'Bear with me, Maxi. We never did do the things I'd planned before. This time we're going to do it right. So

don't waste time arguing, just go and get ready, hmm?
I'll meet you downstairs later,' was all the answer she
got before he vanished once more.

There was little else she could do but follow his advice.
The dress was a perfect fit, she discovered, after she had
slipped into the underwear and applied some make-up.
Fliss had added Maxi's own single rope of pearls to the
collection, and it provided the finishing touch, with her
hair a lush black swath resting on her shoulders. As she
descended the stairs, she felt her heart begin to beat a
little faster.

She found Kerr waiting for her in the lounge, looking
magnificent in his black dinner suit. At her entrance, he
froze, and all her sophistication seemed to leave her when
she saw the warmth in his eyes deepen to a blaze.

'Will I do?'

Kerr crossed to her, framing her face with his large
gentle hands. 'Do? You take my breath away,' he confessed huskily, and brushed a feather-light kiss over her
lips before releasing her. He held out his arm, then, in
olde worlde gallantry, and with a tingle of delight she
took it and allowed him to lead her out to the waiting
car.

Maxi spent the first part of the journey in a nerve-
tingling anticipation. She stared out of the window, but
it was proof enough that her mind was on other things
that it was a good ten minutes before she realised she
didn't know where they were going.

'Are you going to tell me where you're taking me, or
is that a secret?' she asked, not really minding if they
just kept driving forever.

Kerr didn't take his eyes from the road. 'I'm taking
you home, Maxi. Back to where it all started.'

Her lips parted on a silent gasp. 'London?'

Reaching forward, he switched on the radio, filling
the car with soft music. 'Full circle. So just sit back and

relax. There's nothing for you to worry about. Nothing at all.'

She was content to leave it at that, but when she found her eyes kept straying to him she shifted in her seat so that she could watch him more comfortably. It gave her a great satisfaction to know he was hers, that their hearts would belong even if they were worlds apart. It was good to know that someone, somewhere, cared about her.

Kerr didn't drive straight to his house, but to a restaurant tucked away from the main streets. The atmosphere had a friendly warmth, but each table was discreetly secluded with a romanticism that only the French seemed to be able to produce. They were shown to a table by the window, Kerr conversing with the waiter in fluent French. The man then threw up his hands in typical Gallic fashion, turned to her with a beaming smile, and bowed, all the time keeping up a veritable flood of words.

Taken aback, Maxi could only smile and nod, and when he left, turned a questioning face to Kerr. 'I didn't understand a word. What did he say?'

Kerr grinned, reaching across the table to take her hand. 'Roughly translated, he was delighted to see me here with you. He thinks you're a very beautiful lady, and that we make a perfect couple. But, as he could see we were in love and only wanted to talk to each other, he'd leave us alone. You're blushing.'

With a self-conscious laugh, Maxi raised her free hand to her burning cheek. 'It's silly, I know, because he's probably said that to every woman you've brought here!'

Kerr's fingers tightened, and his face was all at once serious. 'I've never brought any other woman here. That's why he was so surprised and delighted. You see, I kept this place for you. I could never have brought anyone else here.'

His confession turned her eyes into sparkling navy pools. 'Never?'

'If that makes me a romantic fool, I don't care. I knew I'd never love anyone the way I loved you. This was to be our special place. I hoped you'd like it,' he went on softly.

'Oh, Kerr, I'm sorry I spoilt it for you by seeming not to be woman you thought I was. I would have liked it as much then as I do now. It's perfect. I'm glad you never brought another woman here. I would have been jealous and hurt if you had!' Maxi exclaimed with a broken laugh. 'It's the sort of place you'd want to come back to each anniversary.'

'It's a little unnerving to discover just how alike we think. That was what I thought the very first time I came here,' Kerr declared, looking about them. 'It has the sort of atmosphere that makes you think anything is possible.'

'I know what you mean,' Maxi agreed, smiling. 'I had no idea you were such a romantic.'

'We never got the chance to find out. Fate was against us that night, but something happened that made it impossible to forget. Perhaps we needed to go through the fire to reach this point in our lives. Something so hard-won has to be special,' he replied gravely.

She stared at him, a tiny frown marring her brow. 'Does it feel special to you, Kerr?' How could she help having some uncertainties, when their struggle had been so bitter?

'Never more so, and by the end of the day I promise you'll think so too,' he told her confidently.

And as the evening progressed, it seemed he was right. There was magic in the air as Kerr wooed her with good food and fine words. He created a world for them that allowed nothing to invade it. This, she knew, was how it should have been, all those years ago. When they left, several hours later, Maxi went into the shelter of his arm easily, feeling cherished. She hummed a tune to herself as they walked back to the car, and it was as natural as breathing to turn up her head to receive Kerr's kiss as he opened the door for her.

The mood lingered as he drove them back to his house, the place where it had all begun. She followed him inside, and when he closed the front door he shut out the real world, locking them into one of their own making. Her heart fluttered, increasing its beat when she looked at him. Kerr smiled, holding out his hand, and she took it, allowing him to lead her down the hall, wishing time could be suspended, and that they could stay like this forever.

She realised where he was leading her, to the conservatory—back to the very beginning. As he opened the glass door, Kerr spoke for the first time.

'It was a long time ago, but it seems just like yesterday to me. I remember looking up, and across the room I saw Columbine. It was as if I'd been struck by lightning. There seemed to be this tremendous energy flowing between us. I'd never felt anything like it before.' Slowly he drew her down the labyrinthine paths to the end overlooking the garden. 'I'd heard of love at first sight, but I'd scoffed at the idea until I met you. It seemed to me that I'd known you forever, and suddenly I felt complete, although I'd never felt a part of me was missing before.'

He halted, and Maxi went into his arms, resting her head against his chest, hearing the reassuringly solid thud of his heart. 'I felt that too,' she confessed softly.

His arms tightened about her, his chin coming down to rub over her hair. 'I knew. I seemed to know everything. We didn't need words, although we spoke volumes. We make each other whole, Maxi. The world, without you, is a colourless place. I love you.'

No one had ever said anything so beautiful to her before. Had she doubted him, then he had just removed that doubt as if it had never been, and she glanced up, her heart in her eyes. 'I love you, too.'

For long seconds his eyes scorched deeply into hers, then he closed them with the touch of his lips, tracing her face until he found her mouth, taking her lips with a gentleness that captured her soul, and sealing them with a vow of eternal devotion.

'Love is all we need. With it we can move mountains,' he declared against her lips.

She eased a breath away. 'When I came back, you were so cold to me, like ice.'

He laughed softly. 'And you were like an angry volcano. It's a much proven scientific fact that heat melts ice, Maxi. I might not have given that impression, but you melted me,' he countered.

'It didn't seem like it to me.'

Now Kerr moved, easing her away so that he could look down at her. 'How could I let you see? I had my pride too. If I'd known then what I do now, it could have been different.'

Maxi frowned. 'How could I tell you? At first I didn't think you had any right to know, and later... I thought I hated you too much to tell you.'

With his thumb he smoothed the crease away. 'Darling, I thought I hated you too, but I soon realised that I couldn't be hurt so much by what I thought you'd done if I didn't still care for you.'

Her smile wavered just a little. 'I never wanted to hurt you, even when I tried to. All I ever really wanted to do was love you!' she exclaimed, choked, and cast her arms about his neck again, burying her face against his throat. 'I wanted you to be the first,' she admitted raggedly, and felt the sudden deep intake of his breath as he realised just what she was saying.

'God knows, I would have been proud to be,' his gruff reply grazed her ear. 'I dreamt of the pleasure we would give each other. Instead of despising you, I should have been suspicious. You needed help, and I could have helped you. When I think of how I abandoned you into his filthy hands... Hell, they can't lock him up long enough as far as I'm concerned!' Kerr growled fiercely.

That made her smile, and she struggled free again, raising her hand to his cheek. 'Don't think about it. Think only of this. You *will* be the first for me. You see, I never felt with him what I do with you. I don't know what physical pleasure is.'

Kerr closed his eyes briefly. 'Then I'll show you, Maxi. It's the most beautiful thing in the world—when two people love each other. I want to love you the way you deserve to be loved. To give you the pleasure that's yours by right,' he declared with an eloquence that made her heart want to burst with love.

He picked her up then, and carried her through the house and up to his room. By the bed he set her on her feet, scanning her face for long seconds before turning her so that he could unzip her dress, pushing it from her shoulders until it fell in a pool at her feet. Gentle hands on her shoulders urged her to face him, and his eyes ran in a brief caress over her body, clad still in strapless bra and panties.

Silently he released her, and removed his own clothes down to his shorts. When she raised a tentative hand to touch him, he held her away. 'Not this time, Maxi. You won't have to do anything. This is for you.' He lifted her again, laying her on the bed and coming to join her. One arm cushioned her head, while the other brushed the hair from her eyes.

Very gently his lips began to explore her face, tracing a line of tender kisses over her brow, her eyes and cheeks, skirting her lips to seek the tender flesh beneath her chin, finding and claiming the rapidly beating pulse at the base of her throat. Maxi caught her breath—she had never been kissed so delicately before—and her lashes drifted down as she slowly relaxed, savouring the new experience.

It was strange how a man's strength could be so gentle, that leashed power held strongly back so as not to frighten or alarm. The brush of his fingers as he released the catch of her bra made her shiver, raising the hairs on her skin and bringing her breasts peaking into hard points. She held her breath, longing for the caress of his hands, but Kerr didn't touch her. Tossing the lace scrap aside, he eased himself away so that he could look down at her, then his fingers skimmed along her arm to her hand, raising it so he could press his lips into her palm.

She blinked up at him then, in surprise, and found him watching her with an intensity that made the muscles of her stomach clench, and her heart leap into her throat.

'You are so beautiful,' he murmured, placing her arm around his neck and finally bringing his mouth down on hers. Yet it was no brutal invasion, but a tender ravishment that urged her to meet him, to join him in this new world they could discover together, and Maxi found herself rising to meet each new caress of his lips and tongue, murmuring incoherent words of pleasure.

But all too soon his lips trailed away, and she gave a moan of disappointment until she felt them moving down over her throat and across her shoulder, with each increased beat of her heart moving closer to where her breasts began to swell and ache for his touch. When finally his mouth closed on her flesh, the shock rocked her, and she cried out in a delight that knifed its way through her body, arching her throat, closing her eyes in helpless wonderment. Unawares, the hands that lay on his shoulders clenched, nails digging into him.

'Oh, Kerr, I . . . don't stop,' she urged, and heard his pure male growl of satisfaction. Her body contracted in instant response to that wild sound.

With her encouragement, he worshipped each swollen globe in turn, arousing in her a response she had never dreamed of feeling before. She began finding it hard to lie still, and her hands spread out over the supple planes of his shoulders. His shudder of pleasure started a throb deep inside her; some deep part of herself was going molten, like lava, heating her up. When she felt him strip away her final covering, she knew only a glorious sense of abandonment. His hands were like hot silk on her skin, gliding over her thighs, soothing her jerk of surprise as they traversed her inner thigh, seeking the core of her.

The gentle caress of his fingers over that most sensitive part of her made her gasp as a spiral of pleasure shot through her, tensing and coiling, building towards a burst of alien delight that arched her back and made her cry out loud.

Her long-drawn-out, 'O-oh!' ended with the brush of his lips on hers, and she opened dazed eyes to stare wonderingly up at him. 'I didn't know anything could fe——' His lips cut off her words, gently bruising hers as they sought and received her response.

'That was only the beginning, my beautifully sensuous love,' he declared with a gasping laugh that set her blood racing.

Her eyes remained locked on him as he rolled from her to shrug out of the rest of his clothes, revealing the aroused perfection of his strong male body, and she held out her arms to him, lips curved in a smile as old as time itself.

Kerr came down on her with a groan, his body trembling in her arms. Yet still he did not let go of that rigid control. He took his time arousing her even further, letting her have the freedom of his body, and Maxi thrilled to his response to her touch. Her heart pounded as she caressed him with all the ingenuity of her love, feeling his heat scorch her as hers did him. Their bodies became slick as they moved together, conducting an electric charge that set the very air around them sparking.

Maxi welcomed the weight of him as he moved over her. It had never felt right before to lie beneath a man.

Because this was *the* man, the one she loved beyond all reason, and when he eased her thighs apart and entered her she felt as if he had taken possession of her very soul. Kerr stopped then, looking down at her. His face was taut with the effort of keeping control, but she wanted him to lose it, to feel the wonderful delirium she felt, so she arched herself into him, moving in silent invitation. Then there was no more time, for at her sign Kerr abandoned that monumental control, thrusting into her with a rhythm she matched eagerly, clinging to him as he bore them both higher and higher on that coil of tension, until finally it broke in a white-hot explosion that carried them way over the edge into their own paradise.

Time stood still for an eternity, until gradually awareness returned. Maxi could hear her heart beating in time with Kerr's, hear the rasp of his breathing as his head lay buried in her shoulder. He was a weight she welcomed, for he had given her pleasure beyond compare. Reverently her hand stroked the line of his spine, until he stirred, lifting himself from her, taking her with him as he rolled on to his back.

Maxi pressed her lips against his firm flesh, and sighed. 'I love you.'

Finding her hand, he brought it to his lips, kissing her palm in a wordless promise. 'I passed the test, did I? Does that mean you'll be staying?'

'If you'll have me,' she joked, and was delighted to feel his chest tremble with laughter.

'I thought I just had, and very satisfactorily too,' Kerr quipped, wincing as her fingers tangled in the hair on his chest. 'Yes, I want you to stay. God knows, I love you more than life itself.'

She knew that, for how else could he have given her so much without thought for himself? 'I was such a fool.'

'We've both been fools for a very long time,' Kerr confessed, curling a strand of her hair around his finger.

'I thought I hated you when you ran off with Ellis. I swore that if we ever met again I'd make you pay for the way you treated me. It seemed to me that every man could have you but me. I was going to put that right, and then I was going to be the one to leave you.'

His confession no longer had the power to hurt her. 'We neither of us knew who the other was. Even had I recognised you, I don't think I would have behaved any differently. I had to do what I did, but I was glad you didn't know. I hadn't thought that you would have fallen in love with me the way I had with you. I thought I was the only one suffering,' she attempted to explain, and felt Kerr's hand curve about her head.

'You suffered more than I did. Perhaps it was justice that I should realise not long after we met again not only that I didn't hate you, but that I still loved you. Anger was the only defence I had against you, but even so you continually got under my skin. Your behaviour confused me, along with all the things you wouldn't say. Knowing the truth, I just wish I could have helped you instead of condemning.'

Maxi raised her head, eyes filled with love. 'I tried very hard not to love you. I knew it would hurt me, because I thought nothing could come of it,' she admitted with a smile. 'You proved me wrong most beautifully.'

Easily he brought her head up to his and for a moment all thought vanished as his kiss stirred the embers of passion. Eventually he forced himself to release her.

'You don't know half the power you have. God help me when you do!' he groaned, and she laughed aloud.

'I'd never use it against you, unless it was to our mutual pleasure,' she teased, and then sighed. 'Did I thank you properly for rescuing me on the Cobb?'

'I should have moved quicker. You're going to be a mass of bruises tomorrow,' he countered ruefully, and Maxi quickly pressed a hand over his lips.

'It is tomorrow, and I don't care. It brought us together where we belong, and for that we should never be sorry, Kerr. I love you.'

He sighed. 'I know, darling. It's all clear now, even that damn stunt when you tried giving yourself to me last night! I was so damn mad when I realised what you were doing, but you'll never know just how hard it was for me to stop. I don't find cold showers in the middle of the night good for my health. I could have strangled you.'

She gazed at him from under her lashes. 'And now?'

In the blink of an eye he rolled over, pinning her beneath him. 'Now, Maxi Ambro, now you pay. For all the sleepless nights you've given me over the last seven years!'

A delicious chuckle escaped her. 'But if I pay you in the way I think you want paying, then that will only lead to more sleepless nights!'

Kerr gave a theatrical groan that didn't match the flame in his eyes. 'I know, but hell, what a way to go!'

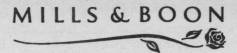

# Next Month's Romances

Each month you can choose from a wide variety of romance with Mills & Boon. Below are the new titles to look out for next month, why not ask either Mills & Boon Reader Service or your Newsagent to reserve you a copy of the titles you want to buy – just tick the titles you would like and either post to Reader Service or take it to any Newsagent and ask them to order your books.

| *Please save me the following titles:* | Please tick | √ |
|---|---|---|
| A DIFFICULT MAN | Lindsay Armstrong | |
| MARRIAGE IN JEOPARDY | Miranda Lee | |
| TENDER ASSAULT | Anne Mather | |
| RETURN ENGAGEMENT | Carole Mortimer | |
| LEGACY OF SHAME | Diana Hamilton | |
| A PART OF HEAVEN | Jessica Marchant | |
| CALYPSO'S ISLAND | Rosalie Ash | |
| CATCH ME IF YOU CAN | Anne McAllister | |
| NO NEED FOR LOVE | Sandra Marton | |
| THE FABERGE CAT | Anne Weale | |
| AND THE BRIDE WORE BLACK | Helen Brooks | |
| LOVE IS THE ANSWER | Jennifer Taylor | |
| BITTER POSSESSION | Jenny Cartwright | |
| INSTANT FIRE | Liz Fielding | |
| THE BABY CONTRACT | Suzanne Carey | |
| NO TRESPASSING | Shannon Waverly | |

If you would like to order these books in addition to your regular subscription from Mills & Boon Reader Service please send £1.80 per title to: Mills & Boon Reader Service, Freepost, P.O. Box 236, Croydon, Surrey, CR9 9EL, quote your Subscriber No:................................... (If applicable) and complete the name and address details below. Alternatively, these books are available from many local Newsagents including W.H.Smith, J.Menzies, Martins and other paperback stockists from 8 October 1993.

Name:................................................................................

Address:.............................................................................

.................................................Post Code:..........................

**To Retailer: If you would like to stock M&B books please contact your regular book/magazine wholesaler for details.**

You may be mailed with offers from other reputable companies as a result of this application. If you would rather not take advantage of these opportunities please tick box ☐